Invitation from Bali

You are cordially invited to...

...a destination wedding! For estranged brothers Ben and Will, the unexpected invitation to celebrate their mother's whirlwind marriage brings up challenges—and feelings—they're unprepared for.

For Ben, having best friend Charlotte by his side is all he needs to cope with his family's drama. But amid tropical cocktails, the shimmering turquoise sea and fabulous sunsets, something between Ben and Charlotte shifts... It breaks all the rules of their friendship, but could it be worth the risk?

Will needs a plus-one and struggling singer-songwriter Summer is the perfect candidate. Why? Because they're complete opposites! Tightly wound Will is all business, while free-spirited Summer is ready for adventure. Which means their watertight contract of pretending to be in love but not actually falling for each other is a deal they can stick to...right?

As warm Bali days lead to hot Bali nights, one thing's for sure—the lives of the Watson brothers will never be the same again!

Ben and Charlotte's story

Breaking the Best Friend Rule

Will and Summer's story

The Billionaire's Plus-One Deal

T0112736

Dear Reader,

Thank you for picking up the second book in my Invitation from Bali miniseries. Don't worry, you can read them in any order; if you haven't already caught Ben and Charlotte's story, you can still enjoy Will and Summer's.

Opposites attract is one of my favorite tropes. I love watching (and writing) two people who think they have nothing in common realize how perfect they are for one another. There's always so much potential for misunderstandings, tension and also humor.

Businessman Will is wound so tightly that one more tweak and he could snap, but he might just have met his match with Summer Bright. Summer is a songwriter and cabaret singer. She's a free spirit and always up for adventure.

I hope you have a fun time watching Will and Summer figure out how much they really do have in common.

Happy reading!

Justine
xx

THE BILLIONAIRE'S PLUS-ONE DEAL

JUSTINE LEWIS

ROMANCE

Harlequin® ROMANCE

ISBN-13: 978-1-335-21604-5

The Billionaire's Plus-One Deal

Copyright © 2024 by Justine Lewis

Recycling programs for this product may not exist in your area.

Harlequin Enterprises ULC
22 Adelaide St. West, 41st Floor
Toronto, Ontario M5H 4E3, Canada
www.Harlequin.com

Printed in U.S.A.

Justine Lewis writes uplifting, heartwarming contemporary romances. She lives in Australia with her hero husband, two teenagers and an outgoing puppy. When she isn't writing, she loves to walk her dog in the bush near her house, attempt to keep her garden alive and search for the perfect frock. She loves hearing from readers, and you can visit her at justinelewis.com.

Books by Justine Lewis

Harlequin Romance

Invitation from Bali

Breaking the Best Friend Rule

Billionaire's Snowbound Marriage Reunion
Fiji Escape with Her Boss
Back in the Greek Tycoon's World
Beauty and the Playboy Prince

Visit the Author Profile page
at Harlequin.com.

For The Usual Suspects
xxx

Praise for Justine Lewis

"Justine Lewis will capture every reader's heart with her poignant, intense and dramatic contemporary romance, *Billionaire's Snowbound Marriage Reunion*. A beautifully written tale...this affecting romantic read will move readers to tears and have them falling in love with both Lily and Jack."

—*Goodreads*

PROLOGUE

WILL WATSON SLID off his tie and threw it on his desk. It was hot, early evening, and sixteen storeys below him the peak hour traffic hummed, but Will still had a few hours of work to do.

He scrolled through his emails searching for the deed he needed. The sun hit his screen and bounced right back into his eyes. He should bring the blinds down. Before he could, there was a knock at his door. His assistant, Belinda, always called through with visitors, so this would be either her or one of his parents. His father, David, had established and still headed up the company, Watson Enterprises, and his mother was a board member. The pair made a formidable duo. Once upon a time he'd wanted a partnership just like theirs. Despite years of wishing otherwise, his chest still ached with the thought that it wasn't to be, but he pushed the feeling to one side, as always.

The visitor was his mother, Diane Watson. She walked around his desk and kissed him on the cheek.

'Hello, darling.' She ruffled his hair. The only person in the world who'd do such a thing. He smoothed it back down again.

'Are you heading home soon?' she asked.

'Not yet. What's up?'

Diane sat across the desk from him. After a pause long enough to let him know what she was about to say was serious, she said, 'Will, we're worried about you.'

'I'm completely fine.' And he was. As long as he could be left alone to finish his work.

'Since Georgia left…'

Not again. This was not the first time Diane had voiced these concerns. It wasn't even the first time this year and it was only January.

'We talked about this.' Yes, his ex-fiancée, Georgia, had broken his heart. But that was years ago. And he was grateful for the lesson she'd taught him. He was stronger and more sensible because of it. He was *fine*.

'Have you thought about hiring a professional?'

'A *what*?'

'Calm down. Someone to talk to. A psychologist.'

Will didn't need a psychologist, or any type of professional. He was perfectly fine. Not wanting a relationship didn't mean he needed help. Being single was a perfectly valid state of being.

'I'm worried you're using work as an excuse not

to have a life. It seems as though you're using work to distract yourself from the pain she caused you—'

'My work—our work—is important. You believe in it as much as I do.'

'I know you have a hard time trusting people. What if I introduced you to some women?'

'No! I really don't need that kind of help.'

The thought of meeting a woman on a date arranged by his mother was mortifying.

'When was the last time you went on a date?'

'Mum, no.'

He had to get back to work or he'd never get home. But his mother looked so concerned. She wasn't going to let this drop.

'Look, Mum, I'm okay. I wasn't going to say anything because it's still early days.'

Diane leant forward. 'You're seeing someone?'

It was late, he was tired and wanted this to end. He nodded.

Diane's face opened into a smile that could have lit up the CBD.

'Who is she? What's her name?'

Will looked out over the city, felt the sweat on his skin from the heat outside. 'Summer,' he said.

'Summer who?'

Through the window the sun still streamed in, hitting his screen. 'Summer Bright. That's her name.'

An image popped into his mind from nowhere. A beautiful woman, surrounded by a halo of hair, golden and fiery. But it was strange this woman had a face; she was a fiction. He'd just invented her and with a name like that she couldn't possibly be real.

'Oh, she sounds lovely,' gushed Diane.

Will stared at his mother.

She sounds made up.

'When can we meet her?'

'It's early days.'

'Sure.'

'And meeting the Watsons isn't a small thing.'

'We're not scary.'

But they were intimidating. David had built a multi-million-dollar plastics company from nothing. His mother sat on half a dozen boards, including companies and charities.

'We can be. *Dad* can be.'

Diane nodded, conceding that David Watson was not always an easy man.

'Well, when she's ready.'

Will nodded and smiled back at his mother. Relaxing back into his chair a sense of relief rolled over him. It was that easy. Make up a girlfriend who his mother would never meet and she'd get off his case once and for all. He was now free to get on with his life just how he liked it.

Alone.

CHAPTER ONE

Two years later...

SUMMER BRIGHT ADJUSTED the straight blond wig. Platinum blonde was definitely not her colour. She had asked to be Frida tonight, her own auburn locks were much closer to Frida's dark curls, but Stacey had arrived first and snagged the brown wig. Summer would be singing Agnetha, the blonde member of ABBA on stage tonight.

They were doing a show in one of Adelaide's largest hotels. It was a fundraiser, but the audience was going to consist of corporate types, drinking bottomless glasses of cheap sparkling wine. They wouldn't be as enthusiastic as a roomful of fans who had only come to hear Summer and her crew perform some classic hits, but once they had a few drinks under their collective belt, they'd get into the spirit of things; alcohol, nostalgia and familiar songs were always a good cocktail for a party. Summer had sung in enough tribute shows to know that, regardless of what someone might say about their musical taste sober and in the day-light, if you started singing a few songs from their childhood, most people would start to sing along.

She had been performing tribute shows for a few years now. The manager, John, started a Beatles tribute show and when that proved suc-cessful, he branched out to others: Fleetwood Mac, Elton John. Summer had joined when he was looking for women to perform in an ABBA line-up. Since then, she'd branched out to Stevie Nicks and Christine McVie and one weekend, when they were short one singer, played a very popular Ringo Starr.

They toured around Australia occasionally, but were now back in her hometown of Adelaide, for which she was glad. She loved travelling, but with her mother's health deteriorating Summer no lon-ger wanted to be far away for long. This job paid well and since she'd lost her guitar her other in-come stream, busking, had totally dried up.

Summer knew the songs by heart and sang them without thinking. On nights like this it was the choreography and the unfamiliar layout of the stage she had to pay attention to.

They were in the ballroom of the hotel, the sort of room that had probably hosted a seminar on the insurance industry earlier that day, so it was not a purpose-built stage. She wanted to stomp her feet hard to 'Knowing Me, Knowing You', but worried her white boots would go right through it. She noticed him first during her solo of 'The Winner Takes It All'.

He was looking right at her. She turned, did a lap of the stage and he was still looking at her. When their eyes met, he looked down.

Did she know him? She didn't know many people well and certainly no one she could think of would be at a gig like this. Corporate fundraiser? The only people she knew here tonight were backstage, serving or performing. No one she knew could pay one thousand dollars a ticket, no matter how noble the cause.

But he looked at her like he knew her. In the half-light, she couldn't make out the colour of his eyes, but there was no hiding his careful, intense stare. His hair was dark, she guessed, and he would also be tall, she guessed, comparing him to the figures sitting around him. Each time she turned, she vowed not to seek him out again, but her eyes kept coming back to him. Did she know him? She was sure she'd remember someone with that sort of presence. Someone who made her tummy flip with simply his gaze.

She turned from him. As she sang the conclusion of the song, the swelling crescendo, the poignant lulls, the song lyrics pushed the handsome man from her thoughts and with each new line about heartbreak and betrayal she thought of the men she'd known over the years. As usual, she was addressing the words to this song to every man she'd ever known.

Brett.

Jason.

Michael.

And her father.

There was a blonde one and a brunette, just like the real ABBA but it was the blonde who caught his eye. There was something familiar about her, but he couldn't place her. It was highly unlikely he knew her; he didn't cross paths with many cabaret singers. Lawyers, bankers, yes. Singers, no.

The evening was billed as 'an immersive dining experience'. It wasn't his first. Dinner shows were part of his job, an occupational hazard, but this was the first ABBA tribute show he'd suffered through.

He didn't hate ABBA, just to be clear, but he did not love ABBA as much as the group of women a few tables down who were singing along and waving their hands in the air.

Attending fundraising dinners, such as this one, organised by his mother, was part of his job as CEO of Watson Enterprises. This evening was for a cause close to his mother's heart: research into ocean preservation. Since Watson Enterprises' main business was now recycling plastics and keeping them out of said oceans, it was good corporate practice to attend events like this. With a big cheque.

The blonde was singing again. The brunette and the two men had stepped to one side, in their white jumpsuits, and the spotlight was on the pretty blonde. Not many people could carry off a white satin jumpsuit, but she definitely could, with just the perfect amount of curves to be interesting.

And she was interesting, her voice strong and full of emotion, undoubtedly. Dark eyebrows framed her bright eyes. Green, he thought. Her pretty cheeks were round, like two half-moons. But something was off. She didn't look like a blonde. No, it was definitely a wig.

He kept watching her because she kept turning to him. Each time she'd turn back to his side of the room her eyes would land on his. With a question. Causing a tightness in his chest.

Did they know one another? Should he recognise her? Will hadn't known so many women so well he'd forget one. Especially not one as captivating as the one on the stage now.

She was singing a breakup song. Unlike with the other songs, the crowd were reasonably subdued, they were watching her, captivated. Listening carefully. This woman could sing. Not only was she hitting the musical notes, but she was also hitting the emotional ones. She sang as though she understood the lyrics. Like she might have written them.

Not angry, but resigned, putting on a brave face. 'The Winner Takes It All.'

Even though he'd heard the song many times before, he'd never really listened. The way she sang the words made him feel the emotion behind the song. The singer was upset, but not bitter.

How did someone reach that level of magnanimity?

His thoughts naturally fell to his ex, Georgia.

He hated Georgia.

He hated what she'd done to his company. What she'd done to his reputation. He hated that he'd trusted her and that because of her, he'd never trust anyone again.

Hate wasn't too strong a word, it was completely appropriate for someone who had seduced him, got him to promise himself to her entirely and then stolen his business plans and sold them to the highest bidder.

As the blonde woman sang he felt a strange sensation in his head. Like she understood.

'Why ABBA?' Will groaned to his mother as they stood in the hotel foyer, looking back into the ballroom where the party was still in full swing. The tribute band had departed the stage, but a DJ was now playing other retro hits.

'It's fun! It gets people in and it gets them relaxed and donating. It could be our most successful fundraiser yet.'

Will couldn't argue with that and it was a very important cause. He was glad it had been a successful night, but he wanted to get home to bed as soon as he could. He had a full day of meetings tomorrow and didn't fancy falling asleep in any of them.

'Besides, I thought you'd like an opportunity to see this particular band.'

Will was lost. 'Why?'

'Oh, I wonder why?' Diane looked at the ceiling as if avoiding his eye, but she was smiling.

In an effort to figure out what on earth his mother was referring to, he looked around the foyer, wondering if the tribute band had left already. Sure, the blonde singer had caught his eye, but surely Diane hadn't noticed. Will was careful to keep his eyes to himself when out in a professional setting and certainly when he was out with his mother. As far as Diane was concerned, Will had been dating a woman named Summer for the past couple of years. Summer was an invention, but served the very important purpose of making his mother believe he was in a stable relationship so she wouldn't worry that he needed fixing. Or worse, needed setting up with some eligible woman his mother knew. Instead of the blonde singer, he spotted his mother's boyfriend, Gus.

Boyfriend. Gus was in his midforties and his

mother was sixty, but Will couldn't quite bring himself to use the word *lover*. Which was what Gus was.

Will's father had passed away suddenly just over a year ago following a stroke. He was glad that his mother was coping well following her husband's death, and Gus was a good man, but Will couldn't help feeling that it was all going a little fast.

His parents had been married for close to forty years. They had been childhood sweethearts and life partners. Within six months of David's passing, Diane had hooked up with Gus. Gus joined them now and kissed Diane on the cheek then held out his hand to Will. The men shook. Diane picked up Gus's hand and squeezed it.

'Darling,' Diane said, turning to her son. 'We have something to tell you.'

Will knew his jaw had dropped, a tell he'd never let himself do in a business setting. He shut his mouth and changed his look to impassive, sensing that he wasn't going to like what his mother was about to tell him.

'We're getting married.'

Diane and Gus smiled at one another like giddy teenagers.

'Why?' Will blurted before he could think better of it.

'I know it may be a shock, but we love one another. It's as simple as that.'

'But…' This was the twenty-first century; people didn't *have* to marry. Particularly not strong, independent women like Diane. The money didn't worry him; Gus and Diane came to the relationship as financial equals. Gus was younger than Diane and not by a little, by over a decade. Still, that wasn't it either.

Gus adored Diane, and Diane adored him. They got along very well.

Will took even breaths.

You should be happy for her.

But his question was a completely legitimate one. Her husband of forty years, the man who was meant to be the love of her life, had recently passed away.

David Watson had been ambitious, single-minded, and talented. A gifted businessman and a driver of change. He had been Will's father, mentor and then business partner. Will missed him every day.

Gus angled his body so he was partly standing in front of Diane. Will resisted the urge to roll his eyes at the protective gesture. His mother could take care of herself.

'Because we love one another, we want to spend our lives together and we want the world to know.'

Will nodded, resigned. It was shock, that was all. He didn't really disapprove; he was simply surprised.

'But you're not going to rush things, are you?'

The couple shared a look and Will's stomach dropped.

'We've booked a date in Bali for three weeks' time. Look, darling, I know it's a surprise, but once the shock wears off, I know you'll be happy for us. We love one another. We're soulmates.'

Like you were with Dad, Will wanted to snap, feeling fourteen years old and a petulant teenager again.

He had the good sense not to give voice to that thought.

He distracted himself by glancing around at the crowded ballroom. Looking for a blond wig.

Which was silly because he didn't know her. He was sure of it. Besides, he had a 'girlfriend'. Summer had a very busy career, just like Will, so couldn't make many family events. He was proud of himself for inventing a name that was so unlikely, no one he knew would ever come across her.

He never intended to lie to his mother, but in a weak, frustrated moment it had just happened. Miraculously, the notion of a fictional girlfriend with the name of Summer Bright had stopped all his mother's attempts to 'fix' him. After everything that had happened with Georgia, falling in love was the last thing he was going to do.

There had been a few hiccoughs along the way. Like when Will realised Diane hadn't kept Summer's existence to herself, but had told several of their friends and colleagues, and the fact that he was dating Summer Bright had made its way to the board who had wanted to know all about her. After the mess with Georgia, he couldn't blame them. When David died and Will was taking over the CEO role, they had sought assurances that Summer had no conflicts of interest that would affect the business.

With some shame and a fair bit of regret, Will had signed a document on her behalf, attesting to this. He reasoned that he wasn't *actually* making a false statement, since Summer didn't exist, and they were not in a relationship, but he didn't want to consider too closely whether a judge would agree.

Requests by Diane to meet Summer were also becoming more and more frequent. Will wasn't sure how much longer he'd be able to last before he parted ways with the improbable Summer. Which was a shame since Summer was the easiest and most convenient girlfriend he'd ever had.

As though his mother had read his mind, she now said, 'I know Summer's busy with work, but it would mean the world to us if she could come.'

'I'll ask her,' Will said, offhandedly. He already knew Summer had some urgent business to attend to. Probably overseas. It was unlikely she'd be able to come at short notice. But why?

Summer had a vague occupation in sales, but

it took her all over the world. She also had her own family responsibilities, something Diane didn't dare argue with. But he'd have to think up something pretty good to get Summer out of the wedding. Family emergency? Dead parent? She'd been 'caught overseas' when his father had died and Diane had been suspicious then. He didn't know how he was going to get Summer out of attending. The thought made him a little sad; his mother and the board were happy with how things were. He was happy with how things were. Breaking up with his fake girlfriend was a last resort.

It wasn't Diane he was worried about, although if she found out he'd lied her campaign to fix him would step up its pace. Will's main worry was the company board. The longstanding board members were his parents' good friends. A few of them were even here tonight. Daniel Jorgensen, the non-executive director, was standing just behind Diane's shoulder, talking to the CFO.

No one must ever find out that he'd made Summer Bright up. The board were already nervy about him taking over as CEO after his father's death. If they found out that he'd lied about this, on top of everything that had happened with Georgia, he could wave his good reputation goodbye. Professionally, he'd be toast. And burnt toast at that.

Summer changed into a long floral skirt and a flowing white blouse to go out to the pub around the corner with her cast mates, an after-show ritual. She'd stay for one drink, then head home to her mother, who, if she was feeling well, would be waiting up. Penny Bright suffered from rheumatoid arthritis and had recently been forced to retire from her job managing a day care centre. Penny coped on her own with most things, but Summer liked being around in case she was needed.

She was making her way across the foyer when she heard her name being called. 'Summer!' yelled her manager, John. 'Summer Bright! Hang on a moment.'

Her shoulders sagged and she walked back across the lobby to where John stood, looking down at his phone. He didn't even look up to say, 'They've cancelled next Saturday's show.'

Summer groaned silently. She depended on these regular gigs to make rent. Busking brought in a little money, but ever since Michael ran off with her beloved guitar, that wasn't an option. There was a real chance she wouldn't make this month's rent. Let alone have enough money to put towards her savings to buy the guitar back. It wasn't just any guitar; it was the guitar her grandfather had owned. The one she'd learnt to play on. The one he'd gifted her. When she played it, she felt closer to him.

And it wasn't just the guitar, it was her busking rig as well. And her car. Michael had taken all three things and skipped town. As far as she knew, he still had the car, but shortly afterwards he'd sold the guitar and rig onto a local man, Brayden from Bowden Park, who had offered to sell both back to her for seven thousand, seven hundred dollars.

Summer never thought there was much chance she'd actually be able to come up with the money, but now there appeared to be none.

'Is there anything else coming up?' Summer asked.

John pulled a face. 'We're doing a show in the hills next week, but I already gave it to the others. If one of them pull out I'll let you know.'

Everyone else was as skint as she was, it wasn't likely anyone would pull out.

With her mother no longer working, Summer would have to try to pick up some more shifts at the second-hand clothes shop she worked at casually, though that didn't pay nearly as well as a night dressed in a retro outfit belting out nostalgia.

As she made her way back across the lobby to the exit a middle-aged woman with a sleek silver bob stood into her path and grabbed her arm. 'Summer? Are you Summer Bright?'

A man rushed up behind the woman and Summer froze. It was the man from the audience and he stared at her intently again now, but this time his eyes were flashing with panic. And silent pleading. Summer looked from one to the other searching for some recognition. But she came up with none. She didn't recognise the woman and her relationship with the man only went back as far as 'The Winner Takes It All'.

'Are you Summer Bright?' she woman asked again.

Who was this woman? Should Summer know who she was? Summer thought she had a good memory for faces, but this woman wasn't ringing a bell. Afraid of what her answer would mean, but also curious to know who the man with her was, Summer nodded slowly.

'I'm so glad we bumped into you. Will is so secretive.'

The woman glanced over to the handsome man who looked at Summer and mouthed something unintelligible to her.

She shook her head once and he repeated the movement. This time she understood. *Play along.*

'Hi!' Summer said, hoping that would suffice.

The woman threw her arms wide around Summer. Surprised by the affection and now doubly embarrassed that she couldn't remember this woman, Summer hugged her back.

When the woman released her from the hug she still held on to Summer's upper arms. Her eyes were bright, even a little misty. 'You don't know how glad I am to finally meet you.'

She was about to open her mouth to ask the

woman what on earth she was taking about when she felt another hand on her forearm.

It was a peculiarly intimate touch for a man she'd only just met, but as the warmth spread up her arm and into her shoulder she relaxed somehow. His touch was just right, pressure perfect. She felt some things uncoil inside her and others tighten.

'Summer, may I speak to you a moment?' he said and she heard his voice for the first time. Low and smooth, it hit all the sweet spots in her chest. But instead of the faraway, dreamy look he'd given her during the show, now the look in his eyes was one of pure terror. When he was ten metres away from her, in the shadows of the audience he had looked gorgeous. But shadows could hide all sorts of things so she didn't think much of it, but now, in the well-lit lobby, she saw that this man was stunning in a stomach-flipping, heart-stopping kind of way. His dark hair was cut close, his strong jaw freshly shaven. He had ridiculously symmetrical cheekbones and deep, deep blue eyes.

He's probably embarrassed that his mother has accosted a stranger with hugs.

'Please,' Summer said, but didn't add, *and tell me what the heck is going on.*

'Always hiding her away. I've met her now, so you no longer have an excuse,' said the woman with the silver bob, still not releasing Summer from her grip. The handsome man's hand was still on her arm, gently but persistently, trying to steer her away from the woman.

Summer was being tugged in two directions. Her mind warned against following a stranger away from a crowd, but her body wanted to go with the man. To somewhere private. To feel his hand slide up her arm. To feel his fingers on the rest of her. To taste him.

Down, girl!

'Excuse?' Summer asked, trying to grasp a thread of the conversation and to decide whether to stay or to disappear into the shadows with this man.

'To come to our wedding! Gus and I are getting married.'

'Congratulations?' Summer looked from the woman to the other man. Also handsome, but older than the first. Wasn't the first man her son? Maybe the woman was unwell. That would make sense. Dementia. Memory loss. The woman wasn't old, but she wasn't young either. Summer knew from caring for her late grandfather that arguing with someone with dementia was pointless and some-times cruel. She wouldn't help this woman by try-ing to set her straight.

The woman touched Summer's hand. 'Please come to the wedding. We're nice people. You'll see. There's no need to be frightened. Will you come?'

'Of course,' Summer said. 'I'd love to.'

'Can I speak to you please,' the man said again in a gravelly whisper that Summer felt in her gut. He smelt good too. Like freshly cut wood. Expensive sheets.

Yes, you can speak to me anytime.

'Make sure you bring her back,' the mystery woman said to the man who was still holding on to Summer's elbow.

Summer wasn't frightened any more, but she was concerned.

'I promise,' Summer said, nodding to the woman but finally giving in to the gentle tugs from the man. Like she'd ever had any choice. She was going to follow him and find out what his hands wanted with her. And how they both knew her name.

'It's so good to meet you!' the woman yelled after them.

The man steered her to a nearby column and he stepped behind it.

Summer was damn well sure she was the only Summer Bright in the world. No one else's parents would give their child such a distinctive name. People often laughed at it, but she thought it was pretty, and it was not easily forgotten. And if she was going to make a name for herself as a songwriter it helped to be memorable. So, what on earth was going on?

Summer looked at the handsome man and then back across the lobby to where the woman was still looking after them. She waved and the other man, the one with the light hair gently turned the woman away. Summer joined the mystery man behind the column and out of view.

'Is she all right?'

'She's fine.'

'She doesn't seem fine. She seems confused. Is it dementia?'

'There's nothing wrong with her. She's sharper, than I am,' grumbled the man.

'Then what's going on? Who are you?'

The man still had his hand on her elbow. Summer wasn't about to run away, at least not until she'd heard the explanation. But she didn't tell him that in case he removed his hand.

'Are you Summer Bright? Is your name really Summer Bright?'

'Yes.' Summer crossed her arms, and the man released his grip. 'Who are you?'

'My name is Will Watson.'

Summer shook her head. Nope. She'd never heard of him.

'Your real name is Summer Bright?'

This was ridiculous. She'd been mocked for her name before, but she'd never come across someone so incredulous. She pulled her driver's licence out of her phone case and shoved it at him.

He studied it.

Summer Angel Bright. Thirty-one years old. And her address. Was he memorising her address? She shivered and snatched her licence back.

'Were you in the show?' he asked.

She nodded.

'The blonde one?'

'Agnetha, yes.' Summer briefly understood how poor Frida and Agnetha must have felt all their lives being labelled the blonde one or the dark one. With light auburn locks, Summer was neither. She was the ginger.

Then he put his face in his hands and groaned. The groan turned into a chuckle and when he finally removed his face from his hands, he looked pained.

'I'm sorry, but should I know you? Who was that woman?'

'That woman is my mother. Diane Watson.'

The name didn't ring any bells either.

'Do I know you? Am I meant to know her?'

'No,' he answered.

'Then why on earth does she think I'm coming to her wedding?'

'Well,' he said, running his hand through his hair. 'It's a funny story. At least, I hope you'll think so.'

'Why does she think I'm coming to her wedding?' she repeated slowly.

'I don't suppose there's any chance you'd like to. As my date?'

CHAPTER TWO

'YOUR DATE? You've completely lost me. Do we know one another?'

He shook his head.

'Is this some kind of prank?'

Will looked down and shook his head. 'No, I'm afraid it's all my fault.' Then he looked up and his blue eyes hit her with enough force to freeze her feet exactly where they were.

'I have a proposition for you. A business proposition.'

This man, Will, had been at the front of the audience. Probably at one of the expensive tables. If he was at this event, he either had money or knew someone who did.

'I'm a businessman. I can get people to vouch for me, if necessary,' he went on.

She wasn't in any business. Except show business.

'You want me to sing?'

'No. Not exactly.'

Alarm bells started to ring in her head. Loudly.

Urgently. 'Nothing about the last five minutes is making any sense to me. I need to get going, it's late.'

'I know it's strange. I was wondering if you would like to come to my mother's wedding. And *pretend* to be my date.'

Summer laughed and turned, but he was after her. Touching her arm again. Not forcefully. Just gently. Sweetly.

'Please, please hear me out, Summer.'

Something about the way he said her name held her back. Familiar. Knowing.

'I'll pay you.'

'That's sounds worse!'

'No, please, it's not that kind of proposal. No funny business. I just need you to come to my mother's wedding and pretend to be my date. And I'll pay you.'

The man clenched his jaw tightly. In fact, it wasn't just his jaw that was clenched tightly. She now could see his shoulders, his neck, everything, stiffen. Wow, this man needed a massage. Or something else.

Not ten minutes ago next weekend's gig had been cancelled. She needed money. Even if the arrangement was unconventional, she should hear him out.

And the sensation of his hand on her elbow did all sorts of strange things to her.

'Why? Why me?' And why does someone as

handsome and breathtaking and warm and sexy as you have to pretend to have a date?

'Now, this is very awkward. I'm sorry in advance for what I'm about to say.' He closed his eyes but didn't look any closer to telling her what was on his mind. He drew a deep breath. 'Do you have a mother?' he asked.

Summer thought of her own mother, probably waiting up back at their flat. 'Yes.'

'And do you love her?'

'Very much.'

'Does she, even though you are an adult, still worry about you? Still want what she thinks is best for you?'

'Yes. But what's your point?'

'This is very embarrassing.'

'So far all you've admitted to is loving your mother. In no world is that embarrassing.'

He opened his eyes. Blue. Bright. Brilliant.

'I told her something I shouldn't have.'

Ah. The puzzle pieces were clicking to place. 'You told her we're dating?'

He nodded. 'I'm afraid so.'

'But you just said we don't know one another.'

'We don't.'

'Then why did you tell her that we're dating?'

The crowd was filing out of the ballroom and the staff were packing the tables up.

'She was putting pressure on me to find a girlfriend.'

It was all weirdly starting to make sense. Except it also wasn't.

'So, I told her I had a girlfriend.'

'You told her *I* was your girlfriend?'

'Not you exactly, I thought I made you up.'

'But I'm a real person. You stole my name!'

'I know that now, and I'm sorry.'

'So, you told your mother you had a girlfriend and you used my name. Why?'

'I can't explain it. I made it up. Or thought I did.'

'You made it up?'

'It sounded…improbable.'

She took a deep breath and let the insult wash over her, but it still stung. It felt like she was back at primary school with kids sniggering about her name behind her back.

'And you want me to go to her wedding?'

He nodded.

The man standing before her had made up a pretend girlfriend and used her name because he thought it was so improbable no real person could have her name. But on the other hand, he'd done it in a bizarre attempt to protect his mother. He was also gorgeous. He was at an expensive fundraiser for the oceans so he was probably a good person. And not the sort of man to steal her guitar and leave the state. But what was in it for her? A free meal? A night out. That wasn't nothing.

And is he part of the deal?

'When's the wedding?'

'Three weeks. But it's in Bali.'

'Bali!' She laughed now. 'I can't get to Bali.'

'I'll pay,' he added quickly. 'I told you.'

'For my flights?'

'Of course, for everything. And I'll pay you for your time. Like a job.'

She'd had some interesting jobs in her time. Tonight, she'd worn a white satin jumpsuit, a long blond wig and sung fifty-year-old songs to a room full of people in business suits.

This would be just like any other job, wouldn't it?

'I can get some references to vouch for me. I'm the CEO of Watson Enterprises. It's a plastic manufacturing company.'

The name meant nothing to her. 'Why don't you just tell her the truth?'

He nodded and then smiled. 'I suppose I could. But I like this idea too.'

She thought she caught a sparkle in his eyes and it did strange things to her belly.

'Besides, you just told her you'd come.'

'Because you told me to play along!'

'Please, think about it. Name your price.'

'Excuse me?' Was he out of his mind?

He might be crazy, but he's offering to pay you. And you need money. Seven thousand, seven hundred dollars to be precise.

'How many nights?'

'Four, maybe five. Whatever you can manage.'

'Seven thousand, seven hundred,' she said, without hesitation. 'Plus, flights and accommodation.' She stood up straight. She'd learnt long ago that no one else was going to look after her, if she needed something she had to get it herself.

'Seven-seven. Are you sure?'

'Is that too much?'

'I've never paid a woman to pretend to date me before. I have absolutely no idea what the going rate is.'

Summer couldn't help but laugh. Despite everything telling her this was all ridiculous, at that moment she trusted Will Watson. He wasn't trying to trick her or do anything underhanded; he was just trying to protect his mother.

But the deal was still…unorthodox.

'What about sex?' she asked.

'What about it?'

'Are you thinking it's part of the deal?'

'I'm not going to pay you to have sex with me.' Colour rose high in his cheeks. 'That's not what this about. I would never.'

'Yes, good.' Heat rose in her own cheeks. 'I thought we should just get that clear.'

'We're not going to sleep together,' he repeated. 'Oh, God, that's not what I'm proposing at all.' His face was now the colour of her lipstick.

'Okay, right, good. But you can't blame me for checking.'

'I don't think we should sleep together. I have

a rule about business and pleasure. A very strict rule.'

'I understand.' She nodded.

The feeling in her gut was nerves, not disappointment. She didn't want to sleep with this man. He was gorgeous, built, tall. And he smelt so good.

But she couldn't want to sleep with him. He was clearly uptight. A businessman who ran a plastic manufacturing company! He was nothing like her.

There would be no sex with this beautiful man who had now let go of her arm, but was standing so close to her, and whose urgent whispers were doing strange things to her chest.

'I'll write it in the contract if it makes you feel better.'

'Yes, it would.'

She sensed that Will Watson was not a man to breach a contract. Which was probably for the best. For many, many reasons.

An all-expenses trip to Bali. She would get her guitar back and all she had to do was pretend to date Will Watson. Every other hesitation melted away.

'Where do I sign?'

'Your next meeting is here,' announced Belinda.

Will stood and smoothed down his suit. It was immaculate and didn't need the attention, but he needed something to do with his hands and with his palms, which were suddenly slightly sweaty.

Was this the silliest thing he'd ever done?

No. *This* wasn't the silliest thing he'd ever done; the silliest thing he'd ever done was not checking whether Summer Bright actually existed before inventing her. Because Summer Bright did exist and now he knew what the twinkle in his mother's eye had been about when she'd hired the ABBA tribute band. His mother had done a search for Summer Bright and had found her. Summer also lived, against all odds and common sense, in Adelaide. Summer's social media showed that she was a singer, songwriter, and performer. And it had only taken a few inquiries for Diane to discover the tribute band Summer performed for and book them for her gala dinner.

Diane had admitted this to Will but said, 'But she's coming to the wedding. You must be happy about that?'

How could Will argue?

If his mother had found the real Summer Bright then anyone could. Including anyone on his board. Since piecing this all together Will knew he was enormously exposed. It was one thing lying about a fictional person, but he'd been lying about a real person. He'd signed a document on behalf of a real person. The thought of his mother and the board members finding out that he'd been lying to them for the past couple of years made him draw a deep breath. He didn't have any choice but to go through with this plan.

Summer strode in and through the floor-to-ceiling windows the sunlight hit her hair. Dark auburn curls framed her face, bouncier than last night. She was wearing brown boots and a long, loose cotton dress. She looked like she'd walked out of a country town, not an office block in the Adelaide CBD.

How had it come to this?

How was he supposed to know that some parents out there were so weird as to give their kid a name like that?

No, it's your fault for coming up with such an extravagant lie.

He could blame his bad luck on Summer happening to walk right past them in the hotel foyer at that time, but one rule his father had instilled in him from a very early age was there was no such thing as bad luck. Only bad planning.

And he had planned the ruse against his mother appallingly.

There were other options. The easiest would have been to whisk Summer away, explain everything and then tell his mother they, sadly, had broken up. But the look on Diane's face when Summer told her she'd come to her wedding had meant that Will had not considered that option until later that night when he was alone and thinking straight for the first time since setting eyes on

Summer Bright. Standing next to Summer, in that hotel lobby, his only thought had been to convince her to come to Bali with him. Her eyes sparkled with amusement and incredulity. Her smile had made her cheeks do that half-moon thing that he'd noticed on the stage and every sensible thought in the world had deserted him.

Summer looked around his office. He'd given himself home ground advantage, but only because Summer held all the cards in this game. If she couldn't convince his family that they were a couple—and had been for about two years—then his lie would be exposed. And his lack of credibility with it.

'Hello and welcome,' he said as happily as he could.

He pointed to the sofas and armchairs. Belinda had put a tray with drinks and pastries on the table for them, but Summer went straight over to the floor-to-ceiling windows and took in the view.

'I can see why you didn't just want to meet in a cafe. Is this actually the tallest building in Adelaide?'

'No, I believe that's Frome Central.'

'Then I guess this is the best view.'

She wasn't wrong. On the horizon to the left was the ocean, to the right the Adelaide Hills. Straight below them were some of Adelaide's famous parks, the Adelaide Oval, and the Botanic Garden.

He had to approach this situation the only way he knew how, like a business deal. And if he were negotiating a deal now, he'd start with hospitality.

'Tea? Coffee?'

'Tea please. Black.'

He poured it for her and hoped his hand wasn't shaking. This was just like any other business meeting. Except that he rarely met with business associates as gorgeous as Summer. Or ones who smelt quite so nice. It wasn't an expensive perfume that she was wearing. Something simple. Natural. He couldn't place it, mixed as it was with the simple smell of Summer.

She took a pastry eagerly and picked the pieces off with her fingers as she ate it.

'Before we start, I just have to ask.' She looked around his office, taking in not just the view but the thick carpet.

Taking in the wealth.

He'd already sussed out that Summer was not materialistic or motivated by money. She was helping him because of his mother, and the amount she'd asked for was preposterous. She must have known that he would have paid much more than eight thousand dollars.

Except she didn't even ask for eight, but seven-seven.

'Why do you have to make up a girlfriend?'

This was not the question he was expecting. 'Like I told you last night, my mother was eager to see me with someone. But my job is my life and my mother doesn't understand that. She wants me to find someone, but I don't want a relationship.'

Please don't ask why not.

'Why not just come clean? Your mother seemed lovely. Wouldn't she understand?'

Summer's question was a good one.

Because if he came clean now, after telling Diane that Summer was coming to the wedding, it would be worse—Diane would *know* he needed help. The pressure to fix him would be even more intense.

'It isn't just my mother. She's on the board of the company. She's told many of the other members I'm in a long-term relationship.'

'How is being in a relationship relevant to your job?'

'It isn't directly, but if it got out that I'd lied, even about this, my professional reputation would be destroyed.'

Summer nodded and chewed on her pastry, thinking it all over.

'What if we just broke up? Why do you need me to go to the wedding?'

Summer made an excellent point. One that a supposedly intelligent person would have realised the night before.

'For starters, you told my mother you would.'

Summer narrowed her eyes.

'And then I told her you were.'

Summer was right, he couldn't pin any of this on her.

'It suits me to not have my mother worry about me. Are you having second thoughts?'

'I'm just trying to figure this all out.'

'You're happy to go ahead?'

'It's an adventure. You're paying me and I've never been to Bali. And I've looked you up. You don't seem like a serial killer.'

'High praise indeed.'

She shrugged and smiled.

'I've looked you up too.' Something he really ought to have done before declaring to his parents that he was dating her. His own research hadn't revealed any red flags. She worked as a singer, she had a diverse group of friends in Adelaide, no one he knew. They moved in very different circles, which was a good thing. There would be little chance of their social lives overlapping. And, importantly, there was nothing in her online presence to indicate she was some kind of corporate spy.

After Georgia he had to be careful about this sort of thing, but in Summer's case, even Will, who was careful to the point of paranoia, had to admit that the chances Summer was trying to trick him were low. This whole thing was a mess of his own creation.

'And?'

'And you don't seem like a serial killer either.'

'Great, we're just regular miscreants then,' she said.

Will's shoulders relaxed. Summer was nice, she seemed like a good person.

He shouldn't be as surprised as he was, but in Will's experience people usually wanted something from him.

'It is a bit ridiculous, isn't it?' he said.

'It's a lot ridiculous, but I'm thinking of it as an adventure.'

She smiled at him and her cheeks turned into small moons again. He felt something snag in his chest. The truth was, there may have been other options. But he liked this one best.

He wanted Summer to come to Bali with him.

'I've taken the liberty of writing up a deed of agreement. I'd rather not get anyone else involved. I trust my lawyer implicitly, but this is different. Personal. Unless you'd feel more comfortable with a more detailed contract.'

He slid the papers across the glass table to her.

'More detailed? This is four pages long!'

'Take the time to read it. If you want to get your own advice on it, that's okay.'

She looked at him like he had two heads.

'What sort of advice?'

'Legal advice.'

She laughed. 'I don't have a lawyer. Do you think I'd agree to be paid to be someone's girlfriend if I had enough money to afford a lawyer?'

'Would you like me to pay for you to get one?'

Summer continued to stare at him like he was from another planet.

'I can read this, and if I have any questions, I'll just ask you.'

'It has the same force as any other contract.'

She nodded, but was only half listening as she read the document he'd put in her hands.

'What's this?' she pointed to the clauses on the second page.

'The times we will meet. The times you will be required on the trip to Bali, obviously. And a preliminary meeting.'

'To get our stories straight?'

'Well, yes, to plan how we're going to do that.'

'You want a meeting to plan the plan?'

He nodded.

'You're joking, right?'

'Of course not.'

'You want a two-hour meeting to plan how we're going to plan?'

'It's one of the first principles of project planning.'

She pressed her lips together like she was trying not to laugh. 'And what are the other principles?'

'Well first, you decide how you're going to plan. And then you plan to assign the tasks and responsibilities, you decide on your outcomes and your KPIs and finally once it's all over you do a post-mortem.'

'A post-mortem? How badly do you think this is going to go?'

'I meant that we debrief.'

'What are our KPIs?'

'There's only one. To make my family believe we're in love.'

He felt her gaze on him again, and his skin warmed. Her eyes were like an X-ray and he was exposed.

Exposed, but not necessarily uncomfortable.

'I do things on the spur of the moment, but I'm sensing you're not the sort of person who does,' she said.

'Why do you say that?'

She picked up his carefully drafted contract. 'Exhibit A, Your Honour.'

'Look, we need to plan how we're going to do this,' he said. 'They think we've been dating for two years.'

'Two years? Two years!' Summer looked like she might stand up and leave.

'Saying it twice isn't going to make it any less real.'

'Why so long? Didn't they get suspicious?'

'Yes, many times. Especially when you didn't come to my father's funeral.'

'I didn't go to your father's funeral? They must think I'm awful.' Summer looked panic-stricken. 'I'm not awful. I would've gone. If we'd actually been dating.'

'I know. But you were overseas. You couldn't make it back.'

'Really, that seems a little callous. Have we had a rocky relationship? On and off?'

'You're away a lot for work,' he admitted.

'Oh, I see.'

'It is what it is, we can't change it now. I understood you couldn't make my father's funeral.'

Summer laughed loudly then caught herself. 'I'm sorry.'

'You don't need to be sorry.'

'No. I'm sorry about your father. If we had been dating, I would've flown back from wherever I was to be with you.'

Will's breath caught in his throat, which was suddenly as narrow as a needle and burning. Even though she was describing a hypothetical scenario, he was in no doubt of her sincerity.

She reached for another pastry, but instead of sitting to eat it, she started walking around his office. She paused at the large canvas behind Will's desk.

'That's amazing,' Summer said.

'It's my brother's. He painted it.' Will felt proud and guilty as he said it. The canvas was nearly two arm spans wide and its intense colours stood out in the otherwise neutral tones of his office.

'It's a beach, isn't it?'

'You can tell?'

'Of course, it might be abstract, but it's clearly

the ocean and a beach. It's beautiful. I love the colours; I can almost taste the sea air.'

Will tasted something as well, but it was bitter. Jealously. 'You don't have to flatter him.'

'I wasn't. I was actually flattering you for having such good taste. Is he coming to the wedding?'

'I'm not sure. I assume so.'

'You're not sure if your brother is coming to your mother's wedding? Don't you talk?'

'Not often,' Will said. Sensing Summer was just the sort of person to want to fix a non-existent problem, he added, 'It's not as though we're not on speaking terms, we just don't talk. We don't have a reason to. We haven't fallen out.'

'He's your brother and you don't talk, but you haven't fallen out?'

'It's complicated,' Will said. He joined her by the painting.

Summer put her hands on her hips. 'Try me. Isn't a complicated relationship with one's brother something a girlfriend of two years might know about?'

'He's an artist.'

'And a good one, I guess. Does he live here?'

'No. He lives in London. I guess that's why we don't speak that often.'

'How long has he lived there?'

'Couple of years. I don't know. Four or five. Before that he was in LA and New York.'

The last time Will had spent any significant

time with his brother had been when they were teenagers. Before Will decided to follow his father into Watson Enterprises. Before Ben decided he didn't want any part of it. Ben and their father had argued, seemingly nonstop from that point. Will didn't want to choose sides, he loved them both. But the simple fact that he had chosen the company annoyed Ben and created a rift between them.

'Have you ever visited him?'

'Nope.'

'If I had a family member living in London or New York or LA, and your kind of funds I'd go and visit them.'

But Summer wasn't him. She was spontaneous. Adventurous.

And Will most definitely was not.

'I have responsibilities here.'

'So do I. But he's your brother.'

Great, Summer might be happy to go along with this little charade, but he sensed that her wish to try to 'fix' him might rival Diane's. Maybe she was right, maybe they should 'break up' now instead.

'Look, Summer, are you sure about this?'

'I'm more certain than ever.'

'Do you want me to pay for a lawyer?'

'Lawyers never helped my mother in any of her divorces.'

'Is that a yes or a no?' he asked.

'If one of us breaks the bargain, then what does

it matter? We'll both lose. How will a lawyer stop that?'

She was probably right. If his family found out the truth, a lawyer could only clean up the subsequent mess.

'Do you have a pen?' she asked.

He took one from the pocket inside his jacket.

Summer spun him around and shoved the paper against his back.

'There are several tables in this room you know,' he said even as he felt the pen press her signature into his back. Like a branding. Sparks shot through his back, into his chest. She spun him back around and handed him the paper.

They were doing this.

'I'll get you a copy,' he said.

'Great.'

'And I'll book our flights and next week I will take you out to discuss the plan.'

'To plan the plan.' She smiled.

'Yes.'

Summer laughed as she left the office.

What had he just done?

CHAPTER THREE

SUMMER READ THE contract on the way home. Four pages of numbered clauses, with subclauses.

She probably should've read it more carefully before she'd been so daring as to sign it across his back, but she'd read the only line she cared about. The one that said he would pay her seven thousand, seven hundred dollars to go with him to Bali for six nights.

The clause that said they wouldn't sleep together was also notable, but reassuring. This was a business deal, nothing more. She'd be required to make his family believe they were in love, but that was all.

The arrangement was not that far removed from an acting gig, which was not too far removed from performing other people's songs. Just like when she performed on stage.

She knew she'd have to tell her mother. She had to explain her absence for a week, but she hadn't quite decided if she'd tell her mother the whole story. Like the getting paid to pretend to be a girlfriend detail. Like everything else in her life, Summer decided it was something she'd make up as she went along.

Spontaneity hadn't worked out particularly well for her but she doubted that careful planning, such as the type Will Watson specialised in, would have put her in any better position. Sure, she didn't have any money. Sure, she lived with her mother, but that would have happened regardless of careful planning.

Planning would not have changed anything in her life. Planning would not have stopped her mother getting sick. Planning would not have stopped Michael stealing her car and guitar. The only way to have prevented that would have been not to have got involved with him in the first place.

Summer's mother, Penelope, was nothing if not open-minded. She was open-minded to the point of vulnerability, which is why the pair of them were now sharing a tiny rented two-bedroom flat.

Her mother had had three husbands and each had left her worse off than the last. Neither Summer nor her mother were any good at protecting their hearts from untrustworthy men. Summer, thinking she'd learnt from her mother's mistakes had been careful with Michael. She'd kept their finances separate, split everything down the middle. Got to know him before they moved in with one another. But despite being careful, he'd still managed to run off with her car and her grand-father's Gibson guitar.

The police were no help, telling her to get a family lawyer. Who would cost more than the cost of the car and the guitar combined. She had to begrudgingly admire Will's attention to detail, but who would have thought there would be four pages of things to put in the deal?

In one week's time, they would meet at Adelaide Airport to board a flight to Denpasar. Business class, the deed said. She would stay at a five-star villa on the island of Nusa Lembongan, all expenses paid by Mr Watson.

Ms Bright, as she was called in the contract, was required to 'maintain the charade that she and Mr Watson had been in a romantic relationship for two years'. Clause five point one.

Ms Bright was not required to have a physical relationship with Mr Watson, 'beyond the occasional gestures in public necessary to maintain that charade'. Clause five point two.

Summer shivered, despite the heat on the stuffy bus. What did the 'occasional gesture in public' involve, exactly? Hand-holding, probably. A hug? A kiss on the cheek? Hopefully. Standing close enough to him that she could smell him? Seeing the humidity on his cleanly shaven chin?

A soft, tender kiss on the lips? All for show, of course.

No. This was a contractual arrangement only.

She didn't know much about Will, but one thing she did know was that business was very important to him. The man was intense. She didn't dislike intensity but thought it would be much better directed at something else. Something fun.

She'd googled Will Watson before going to his office. Will was rich. The internet didn't know exactly how rich he was but he was rich enough to make her kick herself for not adding an extra zero to the amount she'd requested.

Will was the CEO and largest shareholder in Watson Enterprises, one of the country's largest plastic manufacturers. He'd taken over the management of the company after his father, David Watson, had passed away.

Plastic manufacturing didn't sound very ethical to her, which was probably why he was at the ocean health fundraiser. She had to keep remembering this about Will each time she felt a quiver in her stomach and a wish to kiss him: he was a planner, he was uptight, he made money from making plastic! And he wasn't from her world. This was a business deal only. And that was a good thing. In a few weeks she'd have her guitar back and would not have to deal with Will Watson again.

When Summer pushed open the door to her flat her mother was on the couch. Penny made a move to get up, but Summer waved her down. Her arthritis was crippling. Rheumatoid, the worst, most insidious kind that had plagued Penny for much of her adult life but had become particularly worse in the past few years.

'How are you?'

'Fine,' Penny said, though Penny's definition of *fine* was slightly different to Summer's.

'Can I get you a cuppa?'

'Only if you're having one.'

Summer could still taste the one she'd drunk with Will on her lips. She could still smell the expensive office on her cardigan. She boiled the kettle anyway and put bags into two cups.

'I have some news.'

'Bad news?'

'No, good. I think.'

'Then why did you say it like it's bad?' her mother asked.

Had she? No, she was just uncertain about exactly how she was going to explain her weeklong absence to her mother.

'So, a funny thing happened last night after the show. One of the attendees, the organiser in fact, has invited me to Bali for a week.'

'Oh.'

'To go to her wedding.' This wasn't a lie, exactly, Diane had been the first person to extend the invitation. And *technically*, if she was going to be like Will Watson about it, *technically*, she had accepted Diane's invitation.

'And do what? Perform?'

Summer exhaled. 'Yes, perform.' Exactly! 'And they're paying me.'

'Paying your flights?'

'Flights, accommodation, everything. And nearly eight thousand dollars.'

Her mother squinted at her, not believing her. And Penelope was right not to, Summer wasn't telling her the full story. Just a little white lie. So white it was practically translucent.

Penny opened her eyes wide and smiled. 'Eight thousand dollars! That's wonderful. You can get a new car.'

'I was going to buy back Grandpa's guitar.'

'Oh, yes, maybe both.'

Maybe both. Summer kicked herself again for not requesting more money, but it wasn't her way. It was strange enough getting paid to pretend to be Will's girlfriend. Asking for more felt…wrong.

'Bali! You've never been to Bali. It's lovely. Brian took me there once.'

Brian had been husband number two. Unlike Summer's father, who had just been lazy, Brian had actively gambled all of Penny's money away.

'Oh, Summer, are you sure?'

'Mum, it's the best gig I've been offered in ages.'

'Yes, but Summer, think about it. It's not going great, is it?'

'What?'

'You know I've always encouraged to follow your dreams but…'

Summer looked around the flat. It was clean and neat and comfortable. But it was small. She didn't mind living with her mother, but one day Penny was going to need more help than Summer could give her while still supporting both of them.

'I just want more for you than this. Dimity says they're hiring. They need a full-time receptionist. It's steady reliable work. You could still perform on the weekends.'

Summer had tried full-time work once, but it hadn't gone well. She wasn't available to tour so that greatly limited her income. She'd be exhausted by a long week of work and would have to find the energy to perform on the weekend. Most of all, she had no time to write songs. Her main love and passion.

'I do too, but music is my world. I don't want a life without it. That's why I need the guitar and rig. I don't want a job that will suck my soul away. We're doing fine. Especially now. With this trip.'

After Bali, things would be back on track. Her mother would see.

Will had chosen a French restaurant that Summer hadn't heard of, much less dined at. It overlooked one of Adelaide's leafy green parks and the river.

The waiter took her over to a table at the window where Will was already seated. He stood when she approached, flattening his already perfectly ironed suit again. Nervous.

She was getting to know some of his tells, but if they'd been dating for two years, she should probably know a lot more about him than the way he smoothed his suit down when he was nervous. One dinner was not going to be long enough for that.

'Thank you for coming. Would you like something to drink? Champagne?' he said before she'd even had a chance to sit.

She nodded. 'Thank you.'

'Can I take your jacket?' he asked.

She shook her head.

She wore a long pink silky dress. Not actual silk, of course, just silk-like. Nothing she wore had ever seen the inside of a designer store. The straps of the dress were a little tatty and worse for wear but she'd paired it with a silver jacket she'd found at the op shop where she worked. The dress only looked respectable if she wore it with the jacket. She wasn't usually conscious of her clothing, but she was acutely aware of Will's crisp blue suit and smart tie.

As she sat, she took in their opulent surroundings again.

'Do I look okay?' she whispered.

He gave her a confused squint. 'You look beautiful.'

Heat rose in Summer's cheeks and she looked down. 'Thank you. What I really meant was is my clothing appropriate? I don't dress like you, or your mother.'

Will nodded slowly. 'I think you look lovely.' His tone was honest.

'This is how I'm going to dress in Bali, you know.'

'You look great. How you dress is fine. We're pretending to be a couple—I think that's enough. I don't want you to pretend to be someone that you're not.'

Despite his reassurances, worry started to creep in on her. There were so many things she wasn't sure of. While he was no doubt sincere when he told her to be herself, he didn't know her. He had no idea how different they were from one another.

A waiter delivered a bottle of champagne and two glasses to their table. They sat in silence as she uncorked the bottle and poured them both glasses.

'What else have you told them about me? I mean we've been dating for two years you must've told them something more than I'm away a lot for work. What did you tell them I do?'

Will grinned sheepishly. 'I told them you're in sales.'

'Yes, but what does that even mean?'

'It's vague and non-specific, that's why I said it.'

'You do realise I sing in a tribute band? I busk. I work part-time in an op shop. I suppose that could be sales?'

'Yes, I do realise that. And my mother knows

too. She looked you up. I think she booked your band for the charity dinner on purpose.'

'Oh.' Summer had thought their first meeting had just been a wild coincidence, but a meddling mother made more sense.

'She really wanted to meet you.'

'How did you explain never introducing me before this?'

'I told my mother that I didn't want my father to know I was dating a singer. She believed that. And after that, I told her you were busy.'

Summer tried not to be offended at the idea that he felt he'd have to lie to his father about her various jobs.

'I read about your father. I'm sorry,' she said.

'Thank you.'

'He wouldn't have approved of me, then?' Summer took a big swig of champagne. Of course the Watsons wouldn't approve of her. She was a penniless musician. A busker who didn't even own her own busking rig. The Watsons were not her type of people.

'My father was...difficult.'

A ruthless businessman was how her internet search had described him. Will didn't seem to be ruthless. He was uptight, but she'd never got the impression that he was mean. Right now, he was telling her to order anything from the menu she wanted. Three courses. Summer's stomach churned at the prices written in very small font next to the description of the over-the-top-sounding dishes.

'Dad could be critical of things that didn't fit with his plans, Mum isn't.'

Summer bristled again at his use of the word *critical*. There was nothing wrong with her and if he or his family thought there was, then she should just leave now.

'Look, if you have to lie to your family, I'm not sure this is the best idea. If they aren't going to accept the idea of you dating someone like me then shouldn't we just call it quits?' Summer pulled her napkin from her nap and began to refold it.

'Please don't leave. Like I said, the only lie I expect you to tell is that we're dating. I don't have a problem with your career. I think it's interesting. Far more interesting than plastic manufacturing.'

She nodded and re-laid her napkin. For now.

'Yes, yes, it is. Plastic manufacturing? Really? I can't think of anything more dull.'

Her mouth fell at her gall in saying those last words but Will thankfully laughed. 'I agree, it sounds awful. That's what I thought when I was a kid. It's certainly what my brother thinks. But it is more interesting. Really.'

Will then went on to explain that when his father first established the company nearly forty years ago, they made disposable cutlery, cups, and plates, but since Will joined his father over a decade ago, they had pivoted to plastic recycling and making all sorts of products from recycled soft plastics, making Watson Enterprises the largest and most important soft plastic recycler in the country, and awarding his father a posthumous Australia Day Honour for services to the environment.

Before she knew it, they'd finished their entrees. Things had been going smoothly and she'd found herself relaxing. *That's just the wine*, she thought and shook herself back to reality. She shouldn't be trusting him so easily.

'I've talked for long enough. Tell me more about you, tell me about your parents.'

Summer bristled. 'Is this part of the planning?'

'No, it's just part of the getting to know you.'

Her parents were a touchy subject; people always found something to judge, whether it was her missing father or the former two stepfathers who had followed and also disappeared from her life.

'I'm guessing they were alternative types.'

Her hackles were definitely raised now. 'Again why?'

'Well, your name. It's not conventional. I'm sorry, have I said something wrong?'

'There's nothing wrong with my name. If we're going to talk about my name, why did you choose it for your fake girlfriend? Clearly you thought you could date someone with my name?'

'Touché,' he said.

'What made you think of it?'

'I honestly don't know. It was summer. A hot day. You know how hot and bright Adelaide gets in January.'

She nodded.

Will leaned in slightly across the table, his blue eyes drawing her gaze in to his and a gentle smile softening his face. Her stomach twisted. Will was gorgeous and being the subject of his attention was strangely exhilarating.

Wrong. But still exhilarating.

He'll find out all about you eventually.

'My mother worked as a childcare worker, but she's had to give up work as she suffers from rheumatoid arthritis.'

'I'm sorry, that can be an awful condition.'

It was probably because he seemed so understanding at the moment that she added. 'I've no idea where my father is. He left my mum and I when I was three.'

Summer didn't remember her father, but she did remember all the years that followed his departure. He'd left Penny and Summer with nothing but broken promises. Worse than nothing; in the first ecstasy of love he'd convinced Penny to give up her teaching degree, promising to support her. When he left, four years and one child later, Penny had nothing to fall back on and no means to support herself and Summer.

The main thing her father had given her was a

life lesson: you cannot rely on other people, the only person you can depend on is yourself.

'I'm sorry.'

'Mum called me Summer because I was born on the first of December. Nothing more eccentric than that. I like my name. It's memorable.'

Summer might have seemed carefree, even unpredictable, but she knew she had a core of steel when she needed it.

Their main dishes were placed in front of them; fish for her and beef for him. Once they'd nearly finished their mains, he said, 'So, down to business. I suggest we use this time to agree on a list of topics and questions and we will go away and write out the answers. We can study each other's material and quiz one another on the flight over.'

Quiz one another? Was he for real? She didn't say that out loud, but was sure it was written across her face.

'It will give us the best chance of getting to know one another so we don't make a mistake in front of my family,' he added.

Surely the best chance of getting to know one another would be to talk, she thought, but she simply said, 'Of course.' She had to keep remembering he was paying her. This was a job. This was for her guitar.

'But like I said, the only lie we will tell is that we've been dating for two years. I don't want you to pretend to be anyone you're not.'

She nodded but still thought the idea of anyone believing they were a couple was so unlikely it was going to take an Oscar-winning performance to convince his family of that fact.

'So let's agree on some questions then we can go away and write down the answers.'

'Why not just talk about the answers now?'

'If we write them down, we can study them and we're more likely to remember.'

She was going to be earning every cent of this money. Summer took her notebook from her handbag. It was the one she used for writing songs. Will looked at it like it was the first time he'd ever seen paper.

He took out a thin tablet with a keyboard attached, like a mini computer.

'The sorts of things we'd probably know about one another would be things like date of birth, place of birth, who are parents are. Siblings' names and ages.'

Summer dutifully wrote down everything he said.

'And you should also write what you love about your siblings,' she said.

'Why would I do that?' Will asked.

'That's important. I don't have any siblings, but I imagine they'd be important to me.'

Will grunted and typed something into his tablet.

'First memory,' she said. He looked at her

through narrow eyes, but he typed that into his tablet as well.

'School attended,' he said. 'Best subjects at school.'

'Best friends at school and favourite thing to have for lunch,' she added, mostly to spite him.

With a deep, deep sigh Will wrote that in as well.

'Sports played. Final marks achieved.'

Summer resisted the urge to roll her eyes. Who remembered that? People like Will, that's who.

'First crush, family pets,' she said.

'First job.' Will looked at Summer.

'First kiss,' she said, mostly curious about what his response would be. But he nodded.

'Other firsts?' he asked slowly and raised an eyebrow. Muscles she hadn't felt in ages quivered.

'First sexual encounter?' she guessed.

'Only if you're comfortable. Scratch that,' he said. 'No one's going to ask us about that.'

'Yes, yes, of course.' He was right. That was just information she was curious about. 'But we should probably know about any significant relationships the other has had.'

'I suppose so,' he said.

For the first time she was actually enjoying this, but that was probably because it was making him uncomfortable. He thought he had all the answers and all the questions, but there were some things Will Watson couldn't predict.

'Favourite song.' Will said.

'Just one? What about top five ballads, top five dance tunes?'

Will scratched his head. 'How about we just write down as many as we want?'

The man was serious! Write down as many favourite songs as she wanted? 'Favourite movie.' Will said.

'How about top five?' Summer added.

'Of every genre?' Will raised an eyebrow, but she could tell he was kidding. Something inside her chest uncoiled. This may not be as painful as she first thought.

'How about as many as you want to list,' she said with a smile.

'Books?' Will said.

'Same. And ones you've hated.'

She expected that to annoy him but he said, 'Good idea. And same for music and television too.'

This could be a long, messy list. It also had the potential to result in many arguments.

'Favourite food,' Summer said.

'Yes, and allergies and dislikes. Favourite drinks.'

'Worst moment of your life,' she said. 'And the best.'

Will didn't say anything about that suggestion but typed something down.

'Favourite bird,' she said.

'Now you're being silly,' he said.

'No, I'm not. Don't you have a favourite bird?' she asked.

'I can't say I've ever thought about it. What's yours?'

'Magpie,' she said without hesitation.

'Magpie? The stealth bombers of the suburbs?'

'They only do that in spring to protect their babies, but they're highly intelligent and they sing beautifully.'

Will sighed but typed it into his tablet.

With a growing list of things to write about, Will appeared to relax.

'We're going to need a story about how we met. It will be the first thing that anyone asks,' Summer said. 'Or have you already told your mother that?'

Will pressed his lips together. 'I don't...think so.'

She laughed. 'Well think. Because hands-down it's the most important question to have an answer to.'

'How do you know all this?'

'Because when I was in a relationship, a real one, it was what people asked. People are going to assume it's a real relationship until we give them a reason to think otherwise. When was your last relationship?' she asked.

'A while ago. I've been focused on work.'

Summer finished off the last of her lemon tart and spied his tarte tatin. Still half-finished.

'Do you want it?' he asked, picking up on her desire.

'Only if you don't.'

He pushed it over to her.

She could get used to Will and his restaurants and wine.

But she wouldn't. This was a temporary thing only.

'So?' she asked through mouthfuls of cara-melised apple. 'How did we meet?'

'A bar?'

'Nope. We don't go to the same places,' she said.

'Through work?'

'That's even more unlikely, isn't it?'

He nodded. 'Then where would we have met? The beach?'

'I rarely go.' It's not that she didn't like swim-ming, but if she went down to Glenelg or Henley, it was to busk.

'Where do you go, when you're not at work?'

He shrugged.

'Of course. You're always at work.'

'Online?' he suggested.

'Maybe. But honestly, if you'd seen my pro-file online, which way would you have swiped?'

Will looked down, but when he looked up his eyes were earnest. 'If I saw a photo of you, I would have definitely swiped right.'

'And when you read my profile, you would have undone the match,' she said.

He shook his head.

With an uncomfortable feeling in her stomach she said, 'How about the truth? How about you saw me perform in a show? Not the one this week. Obviously.'

'A show? At some dinner?'

'Or you saw me busk. You loved my singing, took my card, and called me up.'

'That'll have to be it.'

She nodded. But even as she did, she knew it was something that Will would never do, even if he lived to be a million years old.

CHAPTER FOUR

AFTER LEAVING DINNER with Summer, Will tried to put their week in Bali out of his mind. He had several things to finish before he went on leave and didn't like the way Summer Bright kept popping into his thoughts at random moments. Like when he was eating his breakfast and thinking about what he would write down for the entry on his favourite foods. Or when he was choosing the playlist for his morning run and wondering what Summer's favourite bands were. What sort of music did she like? Probably old stuff if her ABBA job was anything to go by.

He finished off his answers to the questions they had agreed on the following night. It took him longer than he anticipated, needing to get everything right and ordered, and to give her as much information as possible. The more time he spent on these questions, the less likely anyone would be to guess that they had not been a couple for the past two years.

Still, it was going to be more difficult than he'd

anticipated. Would his family really believe he was dating a singer in an ABBA tribute band? Summer had seen the problem from the very beginning—they were polar opposites. They had an uphill battle ahead of them if this was going to work.

He had the most to lose, his professional reputation. She was just in it for a bit of cash. But despite his resolution to put her out of his mind, he checked his inbox for her response more often than he would like to admit.

Three days out from their trip he was cursing. What was taking her so long? He had to study up on her. He thought about chasing her up, but decided against it.

She held all the cards. Was she not taking this seriously? He couldn't risk Summer revealing the truth. Should he send her a reminder? The little he knew about her made him think that she wouldn't appreciate the nudge.

Should he have offered to pay her more? He'd have paid her whatever she asked. The fact that she'd asked such a paltry sum made him worry. Finally, two days before they were due to leave, Belinda came into the office with a thick white envelope. 'She just dropped it off. Said it was personal.'

'Will Watson' was written across the front in a cursive that looked like it belonged to someone from another time.

She hadn't typed it up like he had, but written by hand. There were at least ten pages, in a beautiful cursive script, telling him about herself.

She'd given away a lot of herself, but he'd just given facts and figures.

Facts and figures are important, he said to himself, but it sounded like his father's voice. When he read the handwritten words, it was only Summer's voice in his head:

My name is Summer Bright. But you know that. Just like you know that I'm thirty-one years old and that my middle name is Angel because you've seen my driving licence. I had to prove to you that I am indeed who I claim to be.

I know you think it's ridiculous, but I've grown to love my name. It's memorable—people always remember me and that's usually a good thing.

Despite my name, my favourite colours are the colours of autumn leaves. Yes, I know I'm cheating—that's yellow and orange and crimson and brown and all the colours in between. Autumn is also my favourite time of year. Unpopular opinion, I know. I can't explain it except that I love the leaves, I love when the air turns crisp. I love wearing lots of clothes, being inside and soups. And because I love dahlias and they mostly bloom in autumn.

I love my job. I love to sing. But more than that, I love to write songs. I'm still trying to make a living from it even though my mother believes I should take a receptionist job with a friend of hers. I tried the full-time work thing a few times and it never really worked. I don't care about the money; in my experience money only complicates things. I only want enough to pay the rent.

Who was this woman? *I only want enough to pay the rent.* What about all the other things money could buy? Comfort? Luxury? Power? Influence? Not to mention food. Concert tickets? Surely those were things she wanted as well.

Boyfriends? Well, that's a story as short as it is pathetic. My last boyfriend, Michael, and I dated for nearly two years. He wanted me to move in with him, but I was worried about leaving my mum. We were trying to find her a new flatmate until I woke up at Michael's one morning. He was gone. And so was my guitar, my busking rig, and my car. To set your mind at ease—as I'm sure you are worried about this—I have no intention of falling in love with you or anyone. I've finally learnt that the only person I can rely on is myself.

Another thing I should tell you is that my relationship with Michael overlapped with 'ours'. I've never cheated on anyone, but in the unlikely event anyone puts two and two together, you should be prepared to know that you were cuckolded. I didn't post much about our relationship, but if anyone asks, Michael was a jerk and we're both glad he's gone.

Damn. He should have thought about this and the fact that the real Summer Bright had been living her life, dating, having relationships for the past two years. Her assurances assuaged his concerns. Besides, it wouldn't be the first time he'd been made to look like a fool in a relationship. He, too, was glad that Michael was gone, he sounded like the bigger fool.

Then followed some pages with her likes and dislikes, in no particular order, just in a stream of consciousness. Likes: soup, bees, magpies. Music of all kinds. Except those with misogynistic lyrics. Fair enough, thought Will.

Dislikes: anchovies, people who are rude and ignorant at the same time.

My dream is to support myself writing my own songs. I love singing but vocal cords age. As do bodies. There will come a day when I won't be able to sing and dance to 'Waterloo' on a shaky stage any longer.

Will touched the page with his index and middle fingers. He was learning so much about Summer from this narrative, some more than his spreadsheet would've taught her. After reading this he felt he knew something about Summer. He didn't understand her but reluctantly admired her. They had very little in common, but Will knew that you didn't need to have a lot in common with someone to be able to do business together.

Summer sat on her bed, legs straight out in front of her, with her laptop resting on them. She clicked on the attachment and waited for it to load. She hadn't opened her laptop in ages, and avoided it whenever she could. All her recordings were on it, but since Michael had bolted with her gear and her livelihood, it was just a reminder of how her life remained frozen. Will, unhelpfully had decided to use a spreadsheet, a type of document she was definitely allergic to. One she couldn't just read on her phone. And this one was a whopper; there were a dozen tabs with titles such as 'Life Story', 'Likes and Dislikes', and 'Relationship History'.

Naturally, she clicked on 'Relationship History' first.

His first kiss had been when he was thirteen with a girl at a school dance. There was a long dry spell, with conscientious Will no doubt focusing on his studies, until university.

She scanned the list, such as it was. First names

only and no one for longer than a few months. There were even phone numbers next to a few of them. She laughed. Was he putting them forward as references?

The list of short relationships also told him he was a commitment-phobe. This wasn't a surprise; he'd confessed to her when they'd first met that he didn't do relationships. She shook her head and clicked on 'Likes and Dislikes'.

His favourite food was chicken burgers and chips. His favourite drink was red wine. His favourite colour was aquamarine. That was more specific than blue or green or red or pink and strangely gave her a glimpse into his mind.

She clicked on 'Life Story' next, but that was nothing much more than a résumé. Where he was born, where he went to school and his work history. His work history was odd: a few casual jobs while he was at school including the usual fast-food outlets, some bar work at university and then straight on to Watson Enterprises, except his time at Watson Enterprises was punctuated by a six-month gap about seven years ago. He probably went travelling or something, but it caught her eye. Where did he go? What did he do? That sounded more interesting than the rest of the 'Life Story' tab. Trust Will to leave the most interesting bits out and focus on the boring parts.

The tab marked 'Entertainment' was the longest of all.

Music, books, movies, all carefully rated out of five. This would've taken him hours.

Was she expected to remember that he gave *The Godfather* three stars? But *The Godfather Part II* five? He liked crime novels, mostly, but read a smattering of sci-fi and a frankly disturbing number of management books.

His favourite movie was *The Princess Bride*. His favourite television show was *The Golden Girls*. Odd, she thought. But she could work with it. His favourite band was U2, which showed a distinct lack of imagination.

She expected the last tab to be something like 'Balance Sheet', but it was blank. Had he created it and changed his mind? What was he going to write?

Will Watson was something else. She just wasn't sure what.

Will paced the departures hall at the airport looking, in vain, for Summer. She'd insisted on meeting him here rather than driving together, which he hadn't thought much of to begin with, but now it seemed like a mistake.

Where was she?

He was a fool, he was relying on her entirely, but she could back out of this deal at any moment. What had he told himself time and time again: Don't rely on anybody else. Don't trust anyone.

Finally, he spotted her red curls, bobbing up

and down outside with the taxis. She was pulling a suitcase out of the boot of a car and waving away help from the elderly taxi driver.

'We're late,' Will grumbled. 'We'd better get going.'

'It's only five past. You said to be here at eleven. Besides the plane doesn't leave for another four hours. We've got heaps of time.'

'Check-In, Security, Customs. They can take hours,' he said.

To Will's great annoyance, they sailed right through all three, barely even slowing down to queue at any stage. Within twenty minutes of Summer's arrival at the airport, they were safely settled inside the business lounge, glasses of French champagne on the table in front of them.

Summer looked lovely. She was wearing soft blue jeans, a white tank top and a loose floral shirt over the top. Her wild hair was loose, but tamed by a small braid holding the front locks away from her face.

Her clothes were always happy and colourful. A lot like Summer. Did she seem nervous? He didn't know her well enough to be able to tell.

The only nervous person here is you.

He took another sip of champagne and felt his head becoming lighter, which didn't usually happen after only a sip or two. It was too late to back out now; they were at the airport. But now he was finally here, the doubts began to creep in. Would anyone believe they were a couple? He could believe that he might fall for someone like Summer; he could imagine asking her out, taking her on a date. Leaning in to kiss her soft dewy cheek…

No. Clause five point two. They would not have a physical relationship. This was a business deal. He was paying her, for crying out loud.

But would anyone believe Summer would fall for him? He knew what people thought of him. Women liked him enough; they flirted with him, asked him out all the time. His mother told him often enough that he was a catch. Why wouldn't Summer fall for him?

He put his champagne glass down. No one was actually going to fall for anyone. They simply had to convince his mother that they had already fallen for one another.

Diane probably knew him better than anyone in the world. She would be able to tell right away that he and Summer had little in common. She'd be able to tell that they hardly knew one another.

They had to get to work.

'Have you been studying?' he said.

'Quiz me,' she said confidently. 'You like swimming in the ocean, but not indoor pools. You say *The Golden Girls* is your favourite show, but you gave every season of *The Good Place* five stars. What's that about?'

'Impressive.' And it was. Even he didn't remember the ratings he'd given to most shows, but they sounded about right.

'I have one question for you though,' he said.

She nodded.

'Why seventy-seven hundred dollars?'

'Excuse me?'

'Why did you ask for seven thousand, seven hundred dollars and not a round eight?'

'Because seven-seven is what I need.'

'What you *need*?'

'Yes. For my guitar.'

'You're going to buy a guitar with the money?'

'Yes, and a busking rig.'

He must have looked as confused as he felt because she added, 'An amp, microphone, you know?'

Will didn't really know. 'A guitar? That's all?' *Must be an expensive guitar,* he thought. Though admittedly he had no idea how much they cost.

'That's what I need. If you'd read my letter you'd know what happened to my last one.'

That was right, Michael the douche of an ex-boyfriend who took her grandfather's guitar, PA system. And her car! She'd told him their relationships had overlapped, but not by how much.

'When did that happen?'

'Three months ago.'

Three months wasn't long, the breakup would still be raw. He wasn't even back at work three months after Georgia left him. He wasn't even thinking straight until a good six months later, and here Summer was, three months later, getting on a plane with a stranger.

She's not with you. This is a job for her. You need to start thinking of it the same way. If the board find out you've lied, this could be the end of you. Your reputation will be destroyed.

'I'm sorry,' he said. 'I didn't realise it was so recent. How are you doing?'

'I'm okay. I've reached the angry stage. Acceptance will come eventually, but right now I'm just furious.'

He couldn't help but smile. 'Did you get another car?'

'No. It's the guitar I need.'

'Shouldn't you buy a car first?'

She groaned. 'You'd get on well with my mother.'

Summer's mother wanted her to get a full-time job, but Summer thought a job would interfere with her music. Even though he'd memorised her letter, he didn't understand her at all.

They sipped their champagne in silence until Summer said, 'That's all? Just one question? I have dozens for you.'

'Like what?'

'Like everything that isn't on your spreadsheet. You answered the questions, but you didn't tell me *why*.'

Why was a big thing for Summer.

'Why what?'

'Why is *The Golden Girls* your favourite TV show? Why is aquamarine your favourite colour?'

'Why couldn't it be?'

'It's very specific. Neither blue, nor green. What's that about?'

'I don't know. It just is.'

Summer sighed deeply.

Will could pass a test on Summer after reading her ten pages, but she might find it hard to talk about him. She'd given him feelings, he'd given her facts, he acknowledged, with a hint of regret.

No. Fact and figures were important. They had to know certain things about one another. They weren't meant to have feelings for one another; they only needed to convince his family that he was not a liar.

'Anything else?' Will crossed his arms.

'Yes. You haven't told me about your mother and Gus. We're about to go to their wedding. What are they like? How long have they known one another?'

'Just over a year I think.'

Summer tilted her head. 'I suppose that's long enough to get to know someone. What do you think?'

'I think no way is one year long enough.' He'd known Georgia for two years. They'd been engaged. And it still hadn't been long enough to really know her.

'Are you worried he's younger than your mother?'

'Why do you think I'm worried about something?'

'Because you're so on edge. You're either gripping that champagne glass like you want to break it or you're gripping the edge of your seat. Are you always this uptight?'

His current mood was more to do with the gorgeous redhead sitting across from him who held his professional reputation in her hands but was treating it like it was a frisbee.

She was distracting. Her hair, her eyes. The sound of her voice. And they needed to be concentrating on facts!

'Do you think he's a gold digger?' she asked.

'Yes, I mean no. I did wonder when they first started dating, but he's actually very wealthy. I don't think he's very materialistic.'

'I agree. He looks like a bit of a hippy.'

Will laughed.

'Is *that* what bothers you? That he's *not* materialistic?'

'Why on earth would that bother me?'

'Because…' She waved her hand in his direction. 'You're so serious, focused on your job.'

'That's not because I need the money.'

She glared at him and for a horrible second he thought she might stand up and leave. He felt his face burn. His last comment was only one that someone who didn't have to worry about money could afford to make.

'I'm serious about my job because recycling plastics and keeping them out of the oceans or landfill is not just important, but critical. And it is a very risky, marginal business. Plenty of companies that have tried to do what we do have failed and ended up in administration.'

'But you're successful—the company is doing well, isn't it?'

Will nodded.

'So surely you can relax?'

He shook his head. She didn't understand. 'You can never relax in business. You always need to keep an eye out. Stay alert for threats.'

She laughed. 'It's a business, not a hunting trip, surely?'

He gritted his teeth. 'I don't think I'm about to get shot, no. But things are always changing, there are always opportunities to take, or miss. If you don't trust the right people, make the right decisions then things can quickly fall apart.'

He didn't want to say any more, he certainly didn't want to tell her about Georgia and how he'd nearly lost his place in the company entirely. He didn't want to tell her how since his father had passed away and he'd taken on the role of CEO he'd felt like he needed to be on guard, on his best behaviour at all times. If the board lost their trust in him, if the shareholders did, then they could lose everything.

'So, no. I don't think Gus is a gold digger,' he said.

'Then what? You're worried about something.' Summer reached over and touched his arm. Electricity shot up it and into his chest. It wasn't unpleasant. It was warm. Exciting.

Summer whispered. 'Tell me more about your father. Not what I can read online, but what he meant to you.'

Who did this woman think she was, his counsellor?

No, she'd just trying to get to know you. She's trying to understand you. And you have to let her.

'Ah…he was amazing. Driven, inspiring and such a natural businessman.'

'You miss him?'

'Every day.' Losing his father had been a double blow, not just losing a parent so young and so suddenly, but losing his business partner and mentor as well. Even now, especially now, he longed to knock on his father's door and discuss something with him. They didn't always agree on everything and his father could be stubborn and set in his ways, but Will never stopped valuing his opinion. Even if it was to disregard it. But his father's office door was now his own office door, and there was no one he had to go to to ask for advice from anything about the volatility of the stock market to what on earth he was going to do about Summer.

'Don't get me wrong, I'm glad Mum has found someone. It's just very soon.'

'People grieve at different rates. He might have been an amazing father and businessman, but it doesn't follow that he was a good husband.'

Will straightened his back. 'My parents were happy.'

'I'm not saying they weren't…but maybe your mother wants to make the most of the time she has left.'

'She's only sixty, she's not on death's door.'

Summer sighed, 'I didn't mean that. Only that people reassess their lives after a death.'

He studied her. She was remarkably composed for someone who had agreed to travel overseas with a stranger and pretend to date them. Like she did this kind of thing every day.

'How did you get to be so wise?'

She shook her head. 'I'm not wise. I want my guitar before a car, remember?' She smiled and his insides uncoiled a little.

And for the first time in days, he dared to think that maybe it would all be all right.

The flight was almost too short, a sentence he never thought he'd hear himself say.

They caught a ferry from Denpasar over to the island of Nusa Lembongan and a small open truck to their villa. If he'd been hoping to have a shower and a stiff drink before facing his family, Will would have been disappointed. Diane was waiting at the villa door for them.

'Here are your keys. Your place is just like Ben and Charlotte's, down the road. Did you really need two bedrooms?'

'I snore. It disturbs Summer's sleep.' Will had already thought of this excuse.

Summer walked over and she slipped her hand in his. He flinched. Her hand was soft and smooth and took him completely by surprise. Diane's eyebrow shot up.

He shouldn't have reacted like that; he should have been happy she was holding his hand. And the thing was, he was happy. He just hadn't expected to like it so much. He hadn't expected the sparks and the pleasure that rolled through him. To show his mother he was utterly at ease with Summer's touch, he slid his arm around her and pulled her close. Her body pressed against his and he was aware for the first time of how wonderful her soft, luscious curves felt against him, how her amazing hair smelt of roses and honey.

'And you know what he's like, he works all hours. I don't want him tapping away on his computer or making international phone calls while I'm trying to get some sleep,' she said.

Diane nodded, but frowned. 'You aren't meant

to be working. This is meant to be a holiday for you, you know.'

'I know,' Will said. 'But the world doesn't stop just because you're getting married. It should, mind you, but it doesn't.'

Diane seemed placated and pulled them both into an extra tight embrace. Will was pressed even closer to Summer and he tried not to let his body tense.

Diane released them from her hug but her hands remained resting on their shoulders. She looked from him to Summer and back again, studying them.

She knows something's up.

A huge smile broke across her face.

'You two are both so beautiful. I'm so glad you're here,' she said and finally let them go.

'Dinner in an hour!' Diane called as she left.

'That was close,' Summer said, letting go of his hand. 'Thanks for arranging two bedrooms.'

'Of course. It was in the contract.' Clause seven.

'Do you think she's suspicious?'

'No, she knows I snore.'

Summer smiled. He liked it when she did. It made something lighten inside him.

'We can't make her doubt that we're physical with one another.' She reached for his hand again and took it in hers. 'You're going to have to get used to me doing that. We don't have to be big on

PDAs but you probably shouldn't flinch if I take your hand.'

Will looked into her eyes. They were warm and kind and he nodded. She let go of his hand and he wanted to grab it back.

Summer looked around their villa and let out a long sigh. 'It's spectacular.'

She wasn't wrong. The main room, with a sofa and dining table opened up onto a spacious deck, also with a daybed, and other chairs. The deck overlapped a crystal-clear infinity pool, its sheen of water appearing to slide off the edge of the pool to the ocean below.

Even though she was distracted by the beautiful view, Summer hadn't forgotten what they'd been talking about moments before. 'How will I know about the snoring if you're in another room? How will I know if you talk in your sleep? How will I know what you wear to bed? Aren't those things a girlfriend should know?'

It had been so long since he'd had a proper relationship, he hardly knew any more.

'Nothing. I wear nothing.'

'Okay, that is good to know.' She coughed and he thought he saw colour rise in her cheeks.

'You?' It was wrong, but he wanted to know. A nightshirt. PJs. Or…like him?

'Just a T-shirt.'

He imagined her in an oversized tee, hair mussed, legs long, lean, and bare and he bit back a smile.

'No one is going to ask you what I wear to bed. Or how long I brush my teeth. Or what I say in my sleep,' he said.

'You speak in your sleep?'

'I've no idea. But it doesn't matter because no one's going to ask.'

As he spoke, he wondered if he was reassuring her or himself.

CHAPTER FIVE

IT WAS WITH no small amount of trepidation that Summer slipped on her bracelets, tied up her sandals and followed Will out into the warm Bali evening to meet his family. She was equipped with nothing more than the facts she'd crammed from an Excel spreadsheet and a deep sense of doubt. She and Will were opposites. He was a planner; she was spontaneous. He cared about money; she cared about music and passion. There was no way his family would believe they were a couple.

She could pretend to be attracted to him, that was not a leap. In Bali, finally out of his suit and tie, Will was different. He'd always been gorgeous. He'd always made a pulse throb in her throat. But in Bali, he was something else. He hadn't shaved, giving his face a slightly more rugged appearance. The moisture in the air gave his hair volume and he hadn't tried to tame it with a comb. Tonight, he wore a linen shirt. It was still buttoned high, but the sleeves were rolled up so she could see his beautiful forearms. Strong, with his muscles and veins for once on view. Acting as though she was physically attracted to Will wouldn't be a hardship. She would barely be pretending.

Pretending to be romantically involved? That was something else.

Watching him walk alongside her, their strides in unison, a strong sense of defensiveness kicked in inside her. Why couldn't they be together? What was wrong with her? Precisely nothing! She was a successful singer. Maybe successful was a stretch, but she made part of her living entertaining people. That was important. Making people happy was a completely noble vocation.

Will *needed* someone exactly like her. Someone fun, someone to encourage him not to take everything in life so seriously. Besides anything else, she was a performer. She had this. She could pretend to be the type of woman Will would fall in love with.

What sort of woman would he fall in love with? Probably someone smart, ambitious, super successful like he was. Corporate, definitely. The spreadsheet had listed half a dozen women, but none of the relationships had lasted more than a few months. Was that long enough to fall in love?

I don't want you to pretend to be anyone you aren't.

But that was just the problem, would anyone believe that Will would love her?

They were about to find out.

The dinner was at a restaurant a short walk up the coast from their ocean front villa. The island of Nusa Lembongan was just to the south of the main island of Bali, a short ferry ride away. There were very few cars on the island, just small open trucks that acted as taxis for the tourists and made the bulkier deliveries. Otherwise, people got around on bicycles and motor scooters. Or they walked, as Will and Summer did now.

Luckily the dress code in Bali was relaxed and casual, perfectly suited to her own wardrobe. She wore a long floral dress and sandals and luxuriated in the tropical warmth.

The restaurant was open and overlooked the ocean, wrapped around by a long wooden deck. Will stopped at the entrance. 'Are you ready?'

She wasn't, but admitting it probably wouldn't help, when she could see that Will was even more nervous than he'd been at the airport. He was pressing his palms down his shirt and shorts. In his button-down shirt, he still managed to look a little too formal. If only she could get him into a T-shirt. Or even a singlet. Or better yet, nothing.

She was about to shake the inappropriate thought away but then realised the sight of her drooling over Will wouldn't hurt the charade. She took his shoulders, spun him towards her and unbuttoned the top three buttons on his shirt. Then she spread her hands across his collarbone, and spread the shirt slightly apart, feeling the strength of his chest under her fingertips. She breathed in deeply. Oh, he was handsome.

'Do you work out?' she asked.

He coughed. 'Only when I have time.'

She raised an eyebrow.

'I swim. Or jog. Most mornings.'

She nodded. 'That would explain it. There's no need to be nervous, it's a completely normal part of going on stage and that's sort of what this is. Once we get out there, it'll be fine.'

Summer reached over and took his hand. Partly for their stage personas, but it felt natural to reassure him. And herself. They *could* be a couple.

She spotted Diane and Gus and they made their way over to them, still holding hands. They all greeted one another with kisses on the cheeks.

'Congratulations again,' Summer said. 'It's so lovely to be here. I'm so excited for you both.'

'No, we're glad that you're here,' Diane said.

Will leant towards her and said, 'Can I get you a drink?'

'Thank you, honey,' she said. So he was going to be a 'honey'. That surprised her; she'd thought he might be going to be a *darling* or a *sweetheart*, but *honey* just came to her tongue out of nowhere.

Will's eyes widened for just a second. 'Rosé?'

'You know it.'

Diane introduced her to her sister who was almost as excited as Diane that Summer was there.

'Oh, Summer, it's so lovely to finally meet you. We were beginning to wonder if Will had made you up!'

Summer feigned a laugh. 'Oh, no. I'm real. And here. And in love with Will.'

The words felt strange crossing her lips.

'We'd almost given up hope of him finding someone.'

Why was everyone so damned happy that Will had a girlfriend? Why were they so obsessed with his relationship status? There was clearly nothing wrong with Will, objectively speaking. He was rich, handsome, intelligent. Maybe a little uptight, but you couldn't have everything. Surely there were many women who would be able to see past Will's quirks to the kind man behind them?

But Will doesn't have a girlfriend, remember? That's why you're here.

'There you go, sweet pea.'

Summer took the wine and tried not to laugh. Sweet pea?

'Summer, I understand we had the pleasure of seeing you on stage the other week,' Gus spoke. 'But Will told us you work in sales.'

Don't pretend to be anyone you're not.

'Yes, I think he thought his family might not approve of him dating a busker. I'm a singer, and sometime songwriter. I sing in tribute bands and travel a little with that. I busk when I can.' *When*

I had a guitar. 'But he didn't fib entirely—I do work part time in an op shop.'

Gus and Diane exchanged a look that made Summer's nerves tighten. It said it all. You're dating a billionaire and you work in an op shop. Pull the other one.

But to Summer's great surprise, Gus said, 'That's fabulous. Second-hand shops are so important. Reusing and repurposing things is so important, don't you think?'

'Yes, of course. I know it seems like Will and I don't have much in common, but love's funny like that.'

'I'm sure you have plenty of things in common. I'm actually impressed that Will found someone like you. It makes me think Will has untapped depths.'

Both Summer and Will reddened. Were there compliments for both of them buried in that remark or insults?

'What do you mean?' Will said.

'Just that I didn't think you were so…imaginative.'

'Imaginative?' Will coughed.

'Yes, I figured Summer would be an ambitious corporate type, a mirror image of yourself. I'm glad to see she isn't. I think you probably complement one another.'

'Summer and I…' Will began and Summer

leant in, desperate to hear him finish the sentence, but Gus cut him off.

'On paper, Diane and I don't have much in common. Many people are confused by the age difference. She's recently widowed. We've had very different lives. We come from different backgrounds. But we have the same values, we can talk about anything and we talk for hours. She's my favourite person in the world.'

Will picked up Summer's hand and squeezed it. They both exhaled in unison.

A couple entered the restaurant. The woman had long dark hair and was amazingly pretty. Summer blinked when she saw the man with her. He was a slightly less handsome version of Will. His hair was lighter. They were about the same height, but the other man was leaner. This must be the brother that Will was so reluctant to talk about, Ben.

'Ben! Charlotte!' Diane greeted them with kisses on both cheeks.

Introductions were made and both Ben and Charlotte greeted Summer warmly with kisses on the cheeks as well. Diane explained that the pair had flown in from London a few days earlier, where Ben was a painter and Charlotte ran an art gallery. They were not, however, a couple, as Summer had initially thought, just good friends.

Charlotte pointed to Summer's jangling bracelets. 'They're so pretty. Where did you get them?'

'Back in Adelaide, but I'm hoping to go shopping for similar things here. I hear they have fantastic markets in Ubud.'

'Yes!' Charlotte exclaimed. 'Ben and I were planning on going tomorrow or the next day. You guys should come with us.'

'That'd be wonderful,' Summer replied. Will glared at her, but Summer straightened her back. Did he want his family to believe they were a couple or not? Besides, Ben and Charlotte seemed like an easier audience than Diane and Gus.

'You have to tell me all about Will,' Charlotte said to Summer. 'Ben is so secretive about his older brother.'

'Likewise!' Summer said, warming to Charlotte instantly. 'I have to drag every detail out of him.'

The guests took their seats and to Summer's horror, Will ended up a few people away from her, sitting with Charlotte. Ben was also nowhere to be found and Summer found herself seated next to Diane. While Diane was lovely, this was going to feel like a quiz show round.

No, Summer thought. She had this. She would turn the tables on Diane. Ask her about Will! Mothers loved to talk about their children. She would hit Diane with so many questions she wouldn't have time to ask any. Summer took a big gulp of wine and went for it.

'I wish I could see some photos of Will as a kid.'

'When we're back, I promise I'll show you.'

'It's so nice to finally meet you all.' Summer looked around the table. 'He's been so secretive about his family.'

'That's probably because of Georgia.'

'Georgia? What happened in Georgia?'

The look Diane gave her filled Summer with dread.

'Not the place. His ex.'

Summer had studied the spreadsheet. She knew his exes. She'd even contemplated texting one of the numbers Will had written down. There had been no Georgia.

'Of course, silly me. He doesn't talk about her much.'

'But he has told you about her?'

'Of course he has. And Prue and Rachel.' Luckily, she could name some of his other ex-girlfriends.

'Yes, well unlike the others, Georgia really hurt him. And then there was the business with the company.'

Summer nodded as if agreeing but she had no idea. 'Of course, yes.'

'I've never seen him so upset as the day he cancelled the wedding.'

Summer nearly choked on her wine. Engagement! She shot Will a look at the other end of the table, but he was laughing with Charlotte. She could have strangled him.

Diane continued. 'I offered to make all the phone

calls but he insisted on doing it himself. It's bad enough to find out your fiancée has betrayed you, but to insist on calling the caterer, the celebrant and everything, that wasn't necessary. It was like he wanted to punish himself.'

'But he'd done nothing wrong.' Summer, who had no idea what had even gone down knew in her heart that Will wasn't to blame.

'No, but he still blames himself. He nearly lost his job. It was only his previous record and yes, nepotism, that allowed him to keep it.'

Will almost lost his job. The CEO of Watson Enterprises almost lost his position?

What on earth had happened?

The question would have to wait and Summer would have to deal with this the best she could, but she suspected that whatever happened with Georgia had something to do with why Will was so anxious for his lie about dating Summer not to be exposed now.

'He's very hard on himself,' Summer said, looking at Will.

But not as hard as I'm going to be on him later for neglecting to tell me about his fiancée.

Diane touched Summer's hand. 'Yes, he is very hard on himself. Too hard. I'm glad you can see that in him. I'm sorry he felt he had to keep you a secret from us for so long. I'm sure he's told you about his father.'

Summer nodded. 'I understand he could be uncompromising.'

'He would have liked you once he got to know you. But David had...views.'

'And I'm a singer. A busker. Not the corporate type he envisaged for his son.'

'No, and thank goodness you're not. Will already had that with Georgia and look how that turned out.'

So, Georgia had been a corporate type. The type of woman that Summer had pictured for Will. The complete opposite of who Summer was.

A strange feeling came over Summer as she sat there, watching the man, his mother's hand warm but gentle on top of hers. The anger she'd felt moments ago was replaced with something else. Empathy. He might be annoyingly uptight, but his outward persona was masking a deep hurt.

Though she was still furious at him for not telling her about Georgia and leaving them both exposed like this. How was she meant to help him if he wasn't honest with her?

Once the plates had been cleared, Summer excused herself from the table and went out to the deck by the dining room for some fresh air and space to think. Behind her, she could hear chattering and excitement. It was such a happy family occasion. It would hurt them to know the truth.

This morning Summer had been in this for the

money, but now she was here it was also very important to her to protect this lovely welcoming family from hurt, especially this week. When the wedding was over, then she and Will would quietly break up and go their separate ways, but Summer did not want to be responsible for ruining what should be the happiest of weeks for Diane and Gus.

Will joined her on the deck and he reached for her hand. She shook his away and hurt flashed across his eyes.

She wasn't sorry.

'You missed a few things on the spreadsheet,' she hissed.

'Like what?'

'Like one fiancée for starters! Like the fact that you were about to be married! Your mother totally sideswiped me with that one. Thanks for letting her ambush me!' Summer turned and walked along the deck, away from him.

Will followed her. 'We can't look like we're fighting.'

'Why not? It's what real couples do, isn't it?' Summer bit out.

Maybe it was, maybe not. She was too annoyed at him right now.

Will looked out across the water and ran his hand through his hair, scraping it back off his high, intelligent forehead.

Gorgeous.

But she was still annoyed.

'Okay, if we are fighting, then we need to make up. That's also what couples do, isn't it?' he said.

'I don't know.' Summer crossed her arms tight. 'I'm not sure I forgive you. You know how much is at risk here.' As an afterthought she added, 'For you.'

He leant in and whispered, 'You do know it isn't real?'

'A sexual relationship might not be, but we do have something.'

It wasn't quite friendship, though it could be. 'We have a business relationship, at the very least. We have to be able to trust one another.'

She crossed her arms even tighter. She was annoyed he hadn't told the truth, but a part of her was also hurt. Which was silly because they weren't even friends. Not really. She'd have to care for him for him to be able to hurt her.

'If you want me to be able to convince them that we're together, you're going to have to start sharing things about yourself. And not just in tabs marked "Entertainment". I'm going to need to know personal things. Like why *The Golden Girls* is your favourite show. Why aquamarine is your favourite colour. And how many ex-fiancées you have!'

She turned away from him and stared out over the ocean, dark except for the lights on the island reflecting on the surface.

'There was only one,' he said softly. 'I'm sorry for not telling you.'

Summer looked from the water and to Will. He looked down at her, earnestly, reached for her hand again and this time she let him take it.

'You should be.'

'I told you about the others.'

He had. But with Georgia it had been different. She had really hurt him. And some implications had followed for the business. Had they worked together? Was that it?

Will turned her hand over in his and studied it, flooding her with happy hormones. His hands were well cared for, and large. One of his could easily hide one of hers. He turned her hand over in his like it was a precious object.

'If they've seen us fight, maybe they should see us kiss and make up,' he said.

He looked at her and her stomach flipped. It would be so easy to lean forward and lift her toes.

But she was afraid of what would happen if she did. And she was still confused by what had happened at dinner.

'I don't know, would it fall within "appropriate physical affection"? I wouldn't want to breach the contract.'

Her hesitation was defensive only. She wanted, she realised with a jolt, to kiss him. But what if she couldn't stop?

Will coughed. 'Yes, I agree. I'm sure a hug will

be sufficient.' He dropped her hand but pulled her into an embrace; she pressed her face against his chest and wasn't prepared for the sensations that swept over her. The hug was no less risky than a quick kiss would have been, maybe more so; Will was strong and solid and she couldn't help burying herself against him. She slid her arms around his back and then up, noticing each muscle in his back; her cheek came to rest on the smooth skin just above the lowest button undone on his shirt. If she moved her lips, she would taste him. If he tasted even half as good as he smelt then she wanted to eat the entire banquet.

He peeled himself gently away and she cursed herself silently for forgetting herself.

Luckily though when she turned to walk back in, she saw Diane watching them both, beaming.

Telling everyone they were tired from their trip, Summer and Will left shortly afterwards and made the short walk back to their villa.

'All things considered, I think that was a pass. It certainly could have gone worse,' he said as he let her into the villa.

'Due to good luck, rather than good management,' Summer said. Will could have taken a pop quiz on Michael and what he'd done to her, but Summer didn't even know of Georgia's existence. Let alone why they had broken up or what the fallout had been.

'Your mother might be more convinced than ever that we're together because she's seen us break up after a fight.'

'We can't mess up again.'

'No, we can't. Which is why you have to be honest with me, Will. You have to tell me about Georgia.'

She said this firmly, though a part of her didn't want to know about the woman who had so clearly broken Will's heart.

'You don't have to tell me everything, but it would help me get to know you. It might also just help.'

Will drew in a deep, resigned breath. 'Do you want another drink?'

'Are you going to talk?'

He nodded.

'Then yes.'

'Is red wine okay?'

'Red is great.'

Summer moved out to the deck overlooking the pool, which in turn overlooked the sea, which was crashing below them against a small cliff.

She sat on one of the deck chairs and Will joined her, passing her a large glass of wine. So, this would be a long story.

He sat in the lounge chair next to her.

'Her name was Georgia. Obviously.'

He was stalling and Summer wished she could make him more comfortable to get his story out.

'I met her through some mutual friends. She was a lawyer, working for a large private firm, and I thought that was great, because she was ambitious, and we moved in the same circles but not too close, if you know what I mean.'

Summer nodded, but she didn't really understand what it was like to be in this world he spoke of.

'She was fantastic, smart, sharp, clever.'

'She was intelligent,' Summer said, teeth grinding together.

Will laughed. 'Yes, and okay, yes, she was gorgeous. Beautiful. Tall, thin, straight long blond hair. She was a knockout.'

Summer's hand went reflexively to her unruly curls, even more unwieldy in the humidity.

Tell me you're not attracted to me without telling me you aren't attracted to me.

'After we'd been dating for about a year, I proposed. I knew she was the woman I wanted to spend my life with. I thought I couldn't have invented a better life partner for me if I tried. She accepted and I thought everything was perfect.'

Will took a big gulp of his wine.

'It's okay, we've all been there,' she whispered, hoping this would make it easier for him to open up.

'I don't know why she did it. I didn't then and I still don't really understand now. Things changed when we negotiated a prenup. It wasn't my idea, but everyone else insisted, including the board. I don't know if she spied a bigger prize elsewhere, if she fell out of love with me. Or if she ever loved me at all.

'She knew about the plan for the new product we were working on. It was a new type of fabric made of recycled plastics, but which can in turn be recycled. She knew enough about all the deals we were setting up with suppliers and buyers. She took the plans to a company overseas. Sold them to the highest bidder and made that other company a fortune in the process, leaving our future plans floundering.'

'I'm hardly an expert, but isn't there some sort of law against that?'

'It's complicated, but any prosecution of her would have also focused on me and the information I'd given to her or allowed her to access, even unintentionally. I'm lucky no one decided to prosecute as it would have made things even worse for me. Even though it meant she got away with it.'

'Oh, Will. I'm so sorry.'

'The board were upset. Actually, that's an understatement, they wanted me fired. It was only thanks to Dad's influence that they calmed down and let me return after I took a few months off. It's taken years to rebuild their trust.'

'You fell in love with her, and then she stole from you.'

Will swung his legs round to stand up. 'When you say it like that, it sounds trite.'

'Sorry, I didn't mean that at all. It's just like what Michael did to me. I was trying to tell you that I understand.'

'The ex who stole your guitar?' Will relaxed back into his chair.

'It wasn't just a guitar—it was my livelihood and my passion. And it was the only thing I had left from my grandfather. You keep saying just a guitar, but to me, it was as significant as what Georgia took from you.'

Will put his face in his hands and was silent for a long beat before he said, 'It wasn't even just the money. It was the shame. The embarrassment, the damage to my professional standing on top of the heartbreak, which wasn't insignificant.'

'I'm so sorry.'

He suddenly looked up from his hands and she felt as though he was seeing her for the first time. 'I'm sorry too. This thing with Georgia was years ago. Michael only left a few months ago.'

She shrugged. She was doing okay, emotionally. 'At this point I'm far more upset about the guitar.'

Will smiled. 'Really?'

'I was hurt, don't get me wrong. But part of me is glad to now know what a jerk he was.'

'That's very sensible. And philosophical. How

do you move past the betrayal? You invested so much in him and he left you with nothing?'

They were strange words to use in respect to a relationship, she thought. 'Love isn't an investment or a business transaction.'

'No, but it still involves give and take. And trust.' Will leant forward and studied her. Under his gaze she felt her body start to sway.

He smiled again and heavens he looked good when he did, his entire aura was transformed from serious businessman to smoking-hot man she'd like to kiss.

She shook herself. No. Love may not be a business transaction, but this was.

'Why do you keep talking about the board, why do they hold so much power? I thought you owned the company?'

'Watson Enterprises is a public corporation. Mum and I own the controlling shares; we own the majority, but we still answer to a board. That's why if it gets out that I lied—even about something like who I'm dating—I'm not sure they'd trust me again. Given what happened with Georgia.'

The enormity of what he was saying hit her. Summer hadn't just come to Bali to protect his mother; she'd come to prevent any risk to Will's professional reputation.

'Then, Will Watson, we'd really better get to know one another.'

He looked up and when their eyes met, his blue bright and brilliant, her tummy did a summersault. They talked and talked. Will poured them both more wine and they sat by the pool. They talked and talked until they lost track of time.

CHAPTER SIX

WILL WOKE TO a gentle knocking at his bedroom door and a slightly heavy head. He had no idea what time it had been when he'd finally stumbled into bed, but knew it had been even later when his thoughts finally slowed enough to allow him sleep.

'Will,' Summer said through the door. 'You've got to get up. We're meeting Ben and Charlotte soon.'

Will groaned and rolled over. They were spending the whole day with his grumpy brother. He wished they could just stay at the villa, relax. And not feel the pressure to pretend.

After last night's long talk, he and Summer were probably new friends. They had talked until after midnight about their lives and he'd told her all about Georgia. It was the first time in years he'd said her name, let alone opened up so honestly about how he'd felt. Summer was a good, calm listener and he was surprised how easy she was to be around.

'Will, do you really want me to come in? I know what you wear to bed, remember?'

He smiled but pulled himself up. Summer liked to take charge, adjusting his clothing. Taking his hand at each opportunity last night. He could hardly complain, these were all normal things a woman might do to a man she was intimate with.

He remembered the way her hands felt on him as she spun him around to sign the contract across his back. How they felt unbuttoning his shirt and smoothing his collar. He felt the muscles tingle across his chest.

He wouldn't put it past her to come barging into his room if she thought they were late.

'I'm up,' he yelled as he swung his legs out of bed.

Will showered and dressed and came out to an enormous fruit platter and thankfully, a large pot of coffee, but Summer only gave him time to gulp down a few mouthfuls before she started hurrying him along again.

'We're late.'

Summer was wearing a short floral dress with thin straps. Her hair was tied up into a loose bun on her head, exposing the pink skin on her neck and shoulders. It would be smooth to touch. Warm to his lips.

But not for you. You made a deal, remember?

'So?' Will said. 'We'll just tell them we slept in.'

'But we'll miss the ferry.'

'You don't understand—we tell them that we *slept* in. It's perfect really. We have an excuse for being late that helps us.'

Summer sighed. 'I suppose so.'

They half ran up the road to the ferry port and saw Charlotte looking at her phone and Ben pacing.

As soon as he caught his breath Will said, 'Sorry we're late,' but Ben frowned.

The two women greeted one another with a kiss on the cheeks.

'We slept in,' Summer said, sheepishly and they exchanged furtive glances. The absurdity of the situation made him crack a smile and then she did too. And next she was giggling.

Ben rolled his eyes. 'Come on then, lovebirds. Try and keep your hands off one another.'

Will's stress levels began to dip, and he felt even more content when Summer reached over and picked up his hand. He squeezed hers. Mostly out of security. As long as they were holding hands no one was going to question their relationship. He liked the way her hand felt in his, not just the security of it but the promise it made. The promise to be by his side. The promise to help. The promise to stand by him.

She's pretending, that's all. None of this is real.

It wasn't real. Because he was paying her, an arrangement that had seemed natural that night in the hotel foyer, but now felt odd.

'Love isn't a business transaction,' she had said last night.

But this wasn't love.

This *was* a business transaction and he took comfort in that. He knew how business worked. It was love he had a problem with.

She's like any other of your employees. Off limits.

Ubud was pretty, but Will didn't enjoy it as much as Ben and the women seemed to, ducking in and out of shops and art galleries. The three of them were definitely in their element. Summer had, he realised with a sad gulp, more in common with his artistic, free-spirited brother than she did with him.

It was all right for Ben to gallivant over the world following his dreams, but Will had responsibilities. To his family. To his shareholders. To the world.

Focusing back on the mission at hand, at least for now, Will was confident that Ben and Charlotte were convinced that he and Summer were, indeed, a couple.

While the women lingered in a craft shop, Ben scuffed his feet outside it. Out of nowhere he turned to Will and said, 'Summer seems lovely. Don't take this the wrong way, but she's not the sort of woman I imagined you with.'

Will's shoulders tensed. 'What's that supposed to mean?'

Ben took a step back, 'Nothing, really. I guess I imagined you with someone more corporate. But it's good really.'

The day was warming up and Will suggested they grab a beer together while they waited. The brothers took a seat on the deck of a small bar overlooking the bustling street.

Over the beers, they chatted about Gus. And their mother. And caught each other up on the goings on of other family members, aunts, uncles and cousins, some of whom would be flying in for the wedding as well. Then Ben said, 'Does Mum not approve of Summer?'

He wouldn't let this go.

'She's surprised. Like you, but she doesn't disapprove. She seems happy I'm dating someone.'

'And was Dad?' Ben asked.

The air stilled at the mention of their father. The man who, more than anyone or anything, was the reason for the current coolness between them. As kids they couldn't have been closer, but as they grew older and it became clear that Will's future lay with the business and that Ben had other plans, the brothers' lives had diverged and they'd become increasingly distant. Did it really have to be like that?

They hadn't spent much time together around the funeral; Ben's visit had been short. He'd spent most of the visit with his mother making the funeral arrangements and Will had been working around the clock, attending to the business implications following their father's sudden passing.

'Dad never met her. You didn't have to have known Dad well to know that he wouldn't have approved.'

'Right,' Ben said, but he didn't sound convinced. He knew something was up.

Will had thought Diane would be the most difficult audience, but it was proving to be Ben. Ben who had barely spoken to him in a decade. Ben who still resented the fact that Will and their father had had a special bond. Ben who, even after all this, seemed to understand Will better than anyone in the world.

They'd grown up together, shared all their childhood secrets and despite a decade of separation it was harder to lie to Ben than anyone. For a crazy second, he contemplated telling Ben everything but stopped himself just in time.

Ben sipped his beer and winked at Will.

What the hell did he mean by that?

No. He had to keep this just between him and Summer. She was the only one he could trust to keep this secret. *Trust. Really? You've barely known her two weeks.* He felt himself slipping, letting down his guard. But he had to remain alert. He couldn't trust anyone, too much was at stake.

They all squished around a small table at lunch, Ben and Charlotte on one side and he and Summer sharing a small bench on the other. Summer's hip pressed happily and reassuringly, against his. The conversation was light, superficial. About the things they had seen, where they would go next. But when Summer got up to use the bathroom, Charlotte leant over the table and said, 'Okay, quick. Spill. How serious are you and Summer?'

Will nearly choked on his pad thai. 'What?' That was not a question he'd rehearsed an answer to.

'You'll have to excuse Charlotte. That was an impertinent question from someone you hardly know,' Ben said.

Will's heart rate began to return to normal, relieved he wasn't going to be forced to answer the question, but a grin grew over his brother's face and Ben continued, 'But a perfectly acceptable question for your brother to ask. How serious are you and Summer?'

Will knew his face was bright red and only partly due to the chili in his lunch. 'We're serious. We've been together for...'

'Yes, years. But you never introduced her before now,' Charlotte said.

First the doubt from Ben about his and Summer's relationship, and now from Charlotte too. Just when Will was beginning to think that the trip was going well. And to top it all off, Summer wasn't here. He couldn't just explain this question away with a kiss.

'I love her,' Will blurted, without thinking of the consequences. Or of how saying those words might make him feel.

I love her.

Something released in his chest as he spoke the words; he felt lighter, freer. Stronger, somehow. Of course he didn't love her. He liked her, very much, as a friend.

I love her.

Will didn't like to lie. He downright hated it. It usually made his heart race and his skin sweat, but once he saw the smile on Charlotte's face, the grin on Ben's and the glance they exchanged, his heart rate in fact, slowed considerably.

It was that easy.

'You'd better bring her to visit us in London then,' Ben said.

Will nodded. At this point it was preferable to go along with whatever they said and not risk anything else. 'That would be great.'

He expected his heart rate to increase, for the sweats to begin at his further lie, but neither thing happened.

'Yes, that would be fantastic. Ben has heaps of room at his place. Oh, you really should visit, Summer's never been.'

Will nodded again. Calmly. He was getting too good at this lying business. It was coming too naturally. Summer slid back into the seat next to him and his heart swelled. He moved closer to her.

He'd missed her thigh pressing against his. Even in the heat, he wanted her touching him. That was so unlike him, but every moment she was next to him he felt content, less on edge.

'They were just asking when we're going to visit them in London.'

'Ahh. And what did you tell them, honey?'

The sound of that term of endearment felt just like that, sweet, syrupy sliding through his veins.

'Soon,' he replied.

'I'd love that.' She smiled at him now and he held her gaze, the pair of them understanding implicitly that the only way to save this situation was to focus on one another and forget that Ben and Charlotte and all of Ubud existed.

It was surprisingly easy to do.

Everything else around him fell away as he felt himself being drawn into Summer's sparkling green eyes. The world dropped away and he could almost imagine what it might be like to take Summer out in London.

Or Paris, or New York. Or even in Adelaide.

Summer was exhausted but strangely exhilarated as they got back onto the ferry. She'd had a fun day, and she'd been enjoying Charlotte and Ben's company so much there were times she'd forgotten why she was there. They were interested in many of the same things she was and it felt like she'd known them for ever and not just barely twenty-four hours.

Her feelings towards Will were more complex.

At times she felt close to him. Felt as though they were becoming friends. But then she had to remind herself that it wasn't real, none of it was. He was paying her to be there. She was no more than his employee. Any intimacy she might feel was simply due to the fact that she was pretending to be his girlfriend.

It was all in her own overactive imagination.

When they boarded the boat, Summer didn't take one of the narrow seats, instead she went to the bow of the boat, hoping a little bit of physical distance between them would help cool the confusing feelings she was having for Will.

Instead of taking a seat next to Ben and Charlotte, Will joined her at the bow of the boat and to her surprise, took her hand. He pulled her close, so close that she could feel the heat from his body and when he spoke into her ear to be heard over the loud hum of the engine, she felt his breath on her neck and a tingle slid down the side of her neck and into her chest.

'I think I may have messed up today with Ben,' he said.

'What do you mean?'

'He said he thought we made an odd couple, he's suspicious I didn't introduce you to my parents before this.'

'Oh, dear.'

Will's brother was right; they did make a very odd couple. This had been Summer's fear from the outset: that they were such an unlikely pairing no one could possibly believe they were together. He worked at the top of a high-rise; she worked on the street. He was driven by balance sheets and the bottom line; he craved order and certainty. She needed the more ephemeral things in life. Music, song, verse. Yet their bodies were inexplicably drawn together.

The salty ocean breeze rippled past them as the boat gently made its way across the narrow stretch of water between the islands.

Summer leant in to whisper into his ear. Would her breath feel the same on his neck as his had on hers, turning him into a quivering mess as his had done?

'It might be time to enact clause five point two,' she said.

When a confused look passed over his face, her heart dropped.

'Clause five point two?'

'The one about necessary physical affection to maintain the charade.'

'Ahh.' Understanding lit up his expression. His mouth was mere inches from her ear. 'What do you think would be necessary?'

'Hand-holding is good. But we've done that, don't you think?'

He nodded slowly and let go of her hand, slipping it instead around her waist. She happily moved her body closer to his, pressed up against him. His body was hard, secure, and steady. She could stand like this all day.

'Like this?' she asked.

'Yes. Are they watching?' she asked as her back faced the rest of the boat.

'Furtively.'

'Perfect.' Summer slid her hand over Will's and up his bare arm. Feeling the firmness of it for the first time; it was warm and smooth and she felt his muscles tense beneath her touch.

'I like that,' Will said and for a second Summer let herself believe that he was referring to her touch and not her performance. But of course, he wasn't.

'It's a good start don't you think? But maybe something a little more. Did Ben sound very disbelieving?' she asked.

'He certainly sounded suspicious.'

His voice sent a wave rippling through her chest and into her belly.

'So maybe something a little more?' Summer shifted her body so that her right foot was between both of his, causing their bodies to be completely flush against the other's. Warm, firm and more excited than she'd felt in years.

Summer whispered into his ear, 'Are they still looking at us?'

'I don't know. If I looked at them, that would spoil everything. I'm supposed to be madly in love with you. I'm supposed to not be able to keep my eyes off you.'

'Good point,' she said.

She felt excited, on a precipice. But if she moved in and kissed him, would it be too much? If she kissed him, would she be able to stop? Summer slid her hand up his arm to his shoulder. She stopped there and waited for a reaction from him, but he didn't move his eyes from hers. Summer slid her hand up the smooth skin of his neck and her fingers slipped into his hair. His eyelids lowered. Their breath mingled.

An actual kiss is just a formality now, she reasoned, and she lifted her lips the remaining millimetres to meet his.

Will's body was immobile against her. It was just a stage kiss. She'd done those before, where choreography required it, and that's all this would be. She moved her lips against his, chaste, tongueless, mouth closed. His arms tightened around her and her knees threatened to buckle.

This was good; this was fine. It was just an act.

Except that the kiss Will gave her back was not a stage kiss; his mouth opened, his tongue sought out hers. Sweeping, swooning, consuming, she opened her mouth to him and dipped her head back to allow Will to deepen the kiss even further. He tasted of the ocean air and escape and everything in her life seemed to click into perfect place. This was where she was meant to be. This was how she was meant to spend her life.

I want to be able to do this with him all the time.

With that thought, she pulled away. The fantasy had clearly overtaken her and was too much for her to handle.

This was *pretend*.

She caught her breath and waited for her heart rate to resume a beat that would allow her to look Will in the eye again.

Whoa.

She'd never in her life had a kiss like that.

If that was what he did when he was pretending, what would it feel like if he meant it?

Will coughed and looked down, also unable to meet her gaze.

Clause five point two.

Wow.

She was in big trouble if that was what clause five point two was going to involve.

Whoa.

Will pulled away from Summer, his head spinning, the floor unsteady beneath his feet. What had just happened?

Clause five point two. Whose idea had that been to agree to physical gestures in public necessary to maintain that charade? That's right. His.

Only the way he'd kissed Summer had gone

far beyond what had been necessary. He'd fallen into the kiss; he'd been the one to open his mouth. He'd taken the kiss to another level. He'd been the one who had breached the contract. Summer looked down. Coughed to clear her throat. She clearly thought they'd gone too far as well.

He stepped away from her but instantly grabbed the railing at the edge of the boat, his knees unsteady, his hands shaking. They couldn't do that again. They had to do everything they could to convince his family they were madly in love without kissing, maybe without even touching. He didn't trust himself to even hold her hand without spinning her into his arms. He certainly didn't trust himself to hug her without sliding his hand around her waist and pulling her soft curves against him.

Most annoying of all when he finally did glance over to where his brother and Charlotte were sitting, they weren't even watching. He'd stepped over a line, risked everything, and for nothing. He had to regroup, get his head together, because right now his thoughts were a scattered mess.

'How about we have a night in? I mean, so we can have a break from pretending.'

He spoke quickly, the words came out in a rush, before he even knew what he was saying.

'I mean, so we can relax and not put on a show.'

Summer's shoulders relaxed. 'That would be great.'

'I can order dinner. If you like. Something local?'

'That sounds perfect,' Summer said, but she turned away from him and looked over the water, to where the ferry was slowly pulling into the pier on Nusa Lembongan. He might want to reach over and place his hand on her shoulder, but he couldn't. If that pretend kiss had proven anything it was just how dangerous kissing Summer for real would be.

CHAPTER SEVEN

SUMMER TRIED TO read the novel she'd brought with her for the trip, but the words bled together. Their kiss kept clawing its way back into her thoughts. And into her body. Was it any wonder? That kiss! Her body tightened just thinking about it, just remembering his arms around her, his hands sliding down her back, and up into her hair. His full lips brushing against hers, their pressure getting heavier and heavier, her being unable to stop her body collapsing against his. His hard and powerful, hers soft, pliant. Willing.

It wasn't just her imagination.

They both should've pulled away much sooner than they did. There was no doubt left in the mind of anyone on that boat that they were into one another.

Summer put the book down and stood. She was hot. Tropical heat plus an impossible attraction? She needed to cool her body down so she could think straight. The sparkling water of the pool beckoned.

She'd packed a sensible one-piece swimsuit—she was here on a professional basis after all. She retrieved it from her case and put in on with some sunscreen, and ventured cautiously out of her room, looking around for any signs of Will. After they had arrived back at the villa, they had both excused themselves. She'd told him she needed a rest and he hadn't argued. Both of them knew they were overdue for a timeout.

Seeing no sign of Will, Summer walked out to the pool.

She sat on the edge and lowered her feet in, the water temperature was just cooler than her body temperature. She slipped gratefully into and under the water, stretching her limbs out into some lazy laps. That was better. The water cooled her body until her brain was thinking straight again. *It's just an act, it's just pretend.* They may have got a little carried away, but they were both healthy, attractive thirtysomethings, was it any wonder? It might be an act, but did that also mean they couldn't enjoy themselves? Was there a rule that said they couldn't?

Oh, that's right there was. Clause six.

Did that mean they couldn't have sex or did it just mean sex wasn't part of the deal?

No, clause six meant No Sex. It was there to protect them both.

Summer looked up from the pool and there he was. Her core temperature spiked again. That wasn't entirely her fault. Will wasn't wearing very much; a pair of shorts, but nothing else apart from a grin. His shoulders were broad, swimmers' shoulders. Of course, since that was his preferred mode of exercise. His pecs were well defined, and his stomach flat and perfect. She turned her eyes away before she looked any lower.

'Hey,' she said, 'I was just getting out.'

'You don't have to. We have some time before dinner.'

'Great,' Summer said, but she scrambled out of the pool anyway.

Clause six. Clause six. She'd be in danger of breaching this contract if she stayed around him half-dressed for much longer. 'I was just going to have a quick shower.'

Summer went to her room and stepped in the shower, turning the water onto its coldest setting. After, she threw on a loose, casual dress, the least flattering item she could find in her suitcase and tried again to read her book while she listened out for the door and their dinner.

The food, a wonderful spread of satays, salads and rice, arrived and was laid out for them on the deck by the pool. She noticed a cold bottle of rosé was delivered with the meal.

Will got out of the water, dried himself off with a towel, then sat at the table as he was. Could he not put a shirt on?

Summer swallowed. Great. Will's beautiful

torso was going to be her dining companion. He poured her a glass of wine and she sipped it, gratefully.

Focus on his face.

Unfortunately, looking at his beautiful eyes made her tummy flip. The sight of his lips just made her think of the kiss...

She focused on her meal. They ate the delicious meal in silence. When the silence changed from companionable to downright awkward, Summer asked, 'What's on tomorrow?'

'I'm not entirely sure, only that Mum told us not to make plans and to bring our party shoes.'

'What do they have planned, do you think?'

'Your guess is as good as mine.'

Summer sighed and looked out at the view. Anywhere but in Will's general direction.

'We've done fine so far,' he said. 'We've had a few bumps, a few close calls, but I think they are believing us. We haven't yet given them a reason not to.'

'Is this a midproject pep talk?'

'Something like that. You covered my not telling you about Georgia—thank you again—and we put on a sufficient show for Ben and Charlotte, that they don't suspect anything.'

'As long as we stay together, we should be able to deal with anything. Do you notice that things go wrong when we're separated?'

'That's true. We'll stick together.'

She made the mistake of turning her focus back from the ocean and he smiled at her. Everything inside her turned upside down.

Summer got up quickly from the table and started clearing the remains of their meal.

'Leave it. I'm not paying you to clean. Let's just sit over there and relax.'

Will refilled her glass and then disappeared to his room, returning moments later wearing a T-shirt.

Summer exhaled.

They sat on the daybeds by the pool and he asked her more about her grandfather and the guitar, and how she got into busking. Will sat forward, attentive as she told him all about how she'd always loved music as a child, how she'd been writing songs since as long as she could remember. He asked her about her writing process, what she loved about performing and despite her earlier resolutions to keep an emotional distance between her and Will, she found herself relaxing into the wine and conversation and the mood.

They finished the bottle and kept talking. When he suggested opening another, Summer was about to say yes, but a voice in the back of her head said, *Keep your distance. Stay professional.*

'I'm actually exhausted and might call it a night. I'm worried about what tomorrow will entail.'

'Yes, that's probably sensible.'

Summer stood and Will mirrored the move.

They stood, facing one another, lit only by a table lamp from a room inside the villa and the moon.

'Thank you for a successful day,' he said.

'You're welcome. It was a pleasure.'

Pleasure? What was she saying. Parts of the day had been awkward, but there were no doubt parts, the part on the ferry in particular, that had definitely involved pleasure.

She stepped towards him, unsure why. 'Goodnight.' She contemplated giving him a quick kiss goodnight. On the cheek only. After the day they had shared it felt strange to part with only a nod. But she stopped herself just in time.

Will reached over and took a lock of her hair between his thumb and index finger. He twisted it through his index finger and studied it closely, as though weighing up two serious options.

Summer held her breath.

He was going to kiss her again.

But he didn't. He sighed and dropped her hair and stepped away.

'It's been a long day. You probably want some time to yourself.'

She did. And yet she didn't.

Summer wanted to see Will Watson lose some control. And then she realised she wanted to be the one to cause it.

And not just for show, but because they both wanted to. Because they both couldn't possibly do anything else.

* * *

Summer woke early, unable to settle her thoughts. Or the stirrings in her bones. There was no way she was getting back to sleep and she was hungry. She hovered outside Will's door. He was inside, probably still in bed.

Probably still naked.

Summer shook herself. Letting her thoughts drift in that general direction was the last thing she needed to do. Especially after yesterday's stage kiss that had quickly spiralled out of control.

It was still early. Diane's surprise event wasn't due to begin until lunchtime. Until then she was on her own. Except not exactly: she and Will had agreed to stick together all day, that way it was far less likely they would raise suspicions. They were stronger together.

But Will was asleep and she was jumpy.

And hungry.

Breakfast and coffee. That's what she needed and when she got back Will would hopefully be dressed. She put on a long skirt and a singlet and let herself quietly out of the villa.

Summer loved Bali. Even if it meant spending the week in a state of suspended sexual tension, she was visiting a beautiful place. She found a small cafe and ordered a coffee. She took out her notebook and opened a fresh page, feeling inspired.

But what to focus the song on? The tension?

The longing? Or the beauty in this tropical paradise? The absolute impossibility of her and Will having anything resembling a real relationship. Because what they had, even the attraction, wasn't real. It was their minds playing tricks on their bodies.

That was all. It happened to actors all the time, as the gossip magazines showed. Every week a new pair of co-stars fell for one another, by the next week they had spilt.

Lost in these thoughts, Summer looked up and saw Charlotte. She waved.

Having breakfast with Charlotte was not in line with their new 'stick together' policy but it was unavoidable. It would look far worse if she didn't ask Charlotte to join her. Charlotte sat down gratefully.

They ordered their breakfast, a delicious chicken and rice for Summer and a sweet Indonesian porridge for Charlotte. As long as she kept the conversation to Charlotte, and not on her and Will, things would be just fine. But Summer had no such luck.

'I just don't know about Ben and Will,' Charlotte said.

'Their relationship, you mean?'

'Yes! What happened? I get the feeling the brothers used to be so close, but then their father was pretty awful to Ben and I think Will was forced to choose. What do you think?'

'I think… I think it's something Will is very touchy about.'

'Exactly! Ben too. But you must know something. What's he told you about his childhood?'

Oh, no…

Charlotte leant forward, eyes wide, obviously expecting a detailed description of the Watson brothers' childhood. She'd asked Will this, but his silly spreadsheet had failed to cover it. There was tension there, though she didn't really understand why. She did know that Will had admired his father very much, though strangely telling Charlotte all these things felt like breaking a confidence, even though it would prove she had a certain level of intimacy with Will.

'He doesn't like to talk much about it.' This was true.

'I know, same with Ben. And I know they both had very different relationships with their father, but they've let it come between them. Which is sad.'

Summer nodded.

'I know Will loved his father. Idolised him.'

'But they were good friends as kids, weren't they? What's he told you about when they were younger?'

Once Summer got out of there, she vowed not to let Will out of her sight until the end of the trip.

'Not a lot. He's really funny about it.'

'And you've been together what, two years?'

'About that. But…'

Charlotte's eyes widened and her jaw dropped hanging on whatever was going to come out of Summer's mouth after 'but'.

If only Summer knew.

'But I know he was happy as a kid. I think the problems with Ben started later, when they were older.'

Charlotte fell back in her seat.

'He does love Ben—I'm sure of it,' Summer added.

'What makes you say that?'

'He has one of Ben's paintings in his office. A huge one. Of the beach. Ben's really talented.'

Summer noticed Charlotte's cheeks redden and she began to wonder if Ben and Charlotte's relationship was really as platonic as Charlotte and Ben both claimed. Summer asked her more and Charlotte confessed that things between the two old friends were complicated, not least because Charlotte had once been engaged to a man who'd died tragically and Summer sensed this was maybe a big factor preventing Ben and Charlotte from being together romantically.

They ate and chatted until Charlotte said, 'Oh, here's Diane.'

'Just the two women I wanted to see. I need you both to come with me.'

Summer thought of Will. *Whatever happens, stick together.* 'I've got to get back to Will.'

'He'll understand. The bride always gets her way three days before the wedding. You leave him to me.'

With a ball of dread in her stomach, Summer followed Diane and Charlotte.

Just like their first night in Bali, Will had trouble drifting off to sleep. Auburn-haired beauties kept creeping back into his consciousness. One auburn-haired beauty in particular. The one who was only two sheets of artistically carved wood away from him in the second bedroom. It was late again by the time he fell asleep and later still when he woke.

It was unlike him to sleep in; usually he was up with the sun for a swim before getting to the office by seven thirty. In Bali his important mission, his one and only job, was Summer. And proving to their family that they were madly in love with one another. And yet he'd slept in.

He pulled on shorts and went looking for her.

He opened his bedroom door to find his mother sitting on the couch, scrolling through her phone. She beamed and stood when he walked out.

'I'm sorry, sweetheart, but I've stolen Summer away.'

'What do you mean?' They were meant to stick together! That was the plan.

Diane laughed.

'Relax, I'll give her back. She's coming to my

hen's afternoon. I want to spend some quality time with her. Get to know her.'

Hen's afternoon? Summer and Diane unsupervised. The lack of control over the situation increased his heart rate. They had agreed to stick together.

'Can I come too?'

'Can't stand to be away from her for a moment?' Diane grinned.

'No. I mean, yes.' Did that question even have a correct answer?

'Well, either way, it's too bad. You're going to Gus's thing. With Ben.'

Will knew he was beaten. He'd have to trust Summer to hold her own. And he could, couldn't he? Summer wasn't silly. He knew her well enough by now to know that she was clever. And wise. After a few near slip-ups, they'd shared more about themselves and were getting to know one another. Maybe not as well as a couple who had been together for two years, but they were more than strangers now—they were becoming friends. Summer would be fine.

He was the one who was going to have the bigger challenge, dealing with grumpy Ben. His brother was physically incapable of looking at Will without a scowl.

'But first, talk to me.' Diane patted the couch next to her.

Will sat down reluctantly. This wasn't going to be good.

'Sweetheart, Summer is lovely. I'm not sure why you kept her such a secret.'

'I…' He couldn't finish the sentence. He'd almost forgotten what lie they were meant to be telling around this.

'I'm so glad we have met her, however inadvertently. I hope it means that you'll spend more time with her,' Diane continued.

'What do you mean?'

'You've been using work as a distraction, as an excuse not to have a life. I hope that will end now that Summer has met your family. Now she can be much more a part of your life.'

Will's heart dropped. Meeting Summer, having her here for the wedding, wasn't the end game. As far as Diane was concerned, it was just the beginning.

'You seem happier.'

He did? He felt uptight. Anxious.

'You're more like you were when you were younger. Before you went into the business.'

Will wasn't sure what his mother was getting at.

'Did it change me that much?'

'It didn't change you exactly, but it brought out certain qualities. Ambition. Drive. All good qualities in moderation.'

What was wrong with being ambitious? It's what his father had always encouraged him to be.

'When you're with Summer, you seem more in tune with what's going on around you. Less like your father.'

His mother's words stung. 'What was wrong with Dad?'

Diane took his hand. 'You know I loved your father. Very much. But he didn't always know how to control his ambition. He didn't have a sense of balance in his life. And I see that with you as well. Ambition is fine, but you shouldn't let it control you. You need to make room for pleasure and kindness in your life too.'

Was she saying he was rude? He never wanted to be unkind. Just the opposite. He wanted to help! Why couldn't anyone see that?

'The business is important. The work is important. Keeping plastics out of the oceans is important—'

'Of course it is. But you know something, so are you. You're important. And you're important and special regardless of what happens to the business. And Summer, bless her, sees that in you.'

For a second his mother's words lit a light in his chest. Summer liked him.

Summer thinks you're special.

Then he remembered his mother only had part of the story. Summer was only *pretending* to like him.

His shoulders slumped and Diane squeezed his hand again.

'I'm sorry you didn't feel as though you could introduce her to us.'

Oh. That's what this was really about.

'I know you think your father wouldn't have understood, but I do, sweetheart. I think she's wonderful and exactly the person you need in your life.'

Will, sadly, was starting to think that too.

It was just his luck. The first person he was drawn to in years was exactly the one he'd agreed to keep his hands off.

Summer watched Charlotte leave the hen's afternoon. She'd been partying with Diane and her friends for the last six hours. They'd enjoyed a long, leisurely lunch at one of the island's upmarket beachfront bars, but Summer had been unable to fully relax, on alert for the constant queries from Diane, her friends and Charlotte about her and Will. Surely, she'd done enough? Served her time. She thought of Will, probably going out of his mind. He'd been peppering her with regular text messages asking how it was going and her answers of Fine, Great and Really, it's all fine hadn't seemed to allay his fears. He sent another saying, Let me know when you're leaving.

Instead of responding, she went over to Diane and told her that she'd be heading off shortly. 'To see Will,' she said. This had the dual effect of making Diane happy and telling Summer to leave.

Back at the villa, Summer was surprised to open the door and find Will, sitting on the couch, a glass of water in front of him, his phone in his hand and a worried expression on his face.

'Hi,' she said. 'I thought you'd still be at Gus's.'

'I thought we agreed to stick together,' he said.

'I know we did, but I could hardly say no to your mother. She made Charlotte and I go and help her set up for the lunch and then put gift bags together for everyone.'

Will rubbed his palm over the stubble on his chin and cheek and Summer wondered what it would feel like to do the same.

'How did it go?' he asked, standing. 'Do they suspect anything?'

Summer stepped towards him and rested her hand on his foreman. 'Relax, it was fine. I just told your mother I was leaving early to come and see you and I don't think I've seen her more excited.'

'There's a "but" isn't there?'

Summer contemplated not telling him about her conversation with Charlotte, but so much was riding on it for him and he could tell she was holding something back.

'I spent a lot of time with Charlotte.'

'Yes?'

'And she was quizzing me about your childhood and Ben's. She thinks there's a big rift between the pair of you and I couldn't answer her.'

Will stepped back and began pacing. 'What did you say?'

'I said you didn't like to talk about it. That I thought you were happy as kids but had drifted apart as you got older.'

'Do you think she believed it?'

'I don't know.'

'So now she'll wonder why I haven't ever talked to you about it.'

'Yes, but I didn't even have to lie. Any time I ask you about your brother, you get your back up.'

'So you think she suspects about us?'

'Look, I just don't know. I answered as best I could. But I do feel you're holding things back. I know we haven't known one another that long, but if this is going to work…'

'I've been sharing things with you.'

'Yes, but only the outline. I don't understand why you're finding it so hard to trust me. I want to help. I don't want to mess this up for you. I really don't.'

It was so strange to admit it, but it was the truth. She'd become so invested in this charade, in helping Will. And in protecting his family. It might have started as a type of job, a way of earning some quick cash, but it had become much more than that.

'This isn't going to work if you don't share more with me about you.'

'There's not much else to say. You've seen the spreadsheet.'

'All that tells me is that you like order. It doesn't tell me much else. I don't know why aquamarine is your favourite colour. You say chicken burgers are your favourite food yet I've never seen you order one. You don't make any sense.'

Will's shoulders dropped and for a moment she thought he was going to turn and walk into his room. But after a few deep breaths he looked her in the eyes and said, 'My favourite colour is aquamarine because it's the colour of the ocean. I don't eat chicken burgers, or any fast food, because my father died of a stroke aged sixty. And my favourite television show is *The Golden Girls* because I watched it with my grandmother. Are you happy now?'

Charlotte bit her lip to stop herself smiling. Her heart was melting and she wanted to hug him. But he wasn't done.

'And?'

Will looked skyward. 'And Ben and I used to be so close, but as we got older Dad hated the fact that Ben didn't want to join the business, he saw it as a type of rejection. Ben was hurt by his reaction and I was stuck in the middle. I should have made more of an effort to maintain my relationship with Ben, but I was a foolish young kid and I didn't and I regret it. And I'm not sure how to make it up.'

Summer walked up to him and kissed him on the lips.

She shocked even herself with her audacity and pulled back slightly. His eyes were wide, pupils dilated. Full of shock. She expected him to push her away. But he didn't. He wrapped his arms around her and pressed his mouth back on hers. Her lips parted, her body fell into his, remembering the kiss on the boat, needing him, wanting, with every cell in her body, to be wrapped up completely with him.

Their lips tugged and pushed, pressed, and teased. She felt his hands slide up her back, into her hair. She felt his body harden, the air in the room shifted.

Everything had changed.

CHAPTER EIGHT

IT WOULD'VE BEEN easier to fly under his own steam than tear himself away from Summer. Will needed her lips like he needed air. Surrounded by her touch, her scent, he didn't know which way was up.

But eventually the pounding in his veins, the throbbing of his body and the feeling that his legs might give way from the lack of air, made him pull back slightly.

And when he did, the spell was broken.

Panting, Summer stepped back and looked away.

That was amazing, he wanted to say. But good sense stopped him. It might have been amazing, but it wasn't part of their deal. He'd crossed a line and he wouldn't blame her for walking out right now.

She kissed you first, remember?

Yes, but the kiss Summer had given him had been a chaste peck compared with the full-body ravishing he'd just given her.

'I'm so sorry—I don't know what came over me,' he said.

'We just got confused. That's all. It's natural when you're playing a part, isn't it?' She was still catching her breath.

She was the performer, she would know.

'So, we should scratch it up to a blurring of our roles? Taking our act too seriously?' he asked. He wasn't an actor; he'd never even been comfortable stretching the truth. The kiss had felt real to him. As real as any other kiss he'd ever had, if not more so.

His body had taken over, his heart had expanded and rational thought was an afterthought. He didn't want to let her go, for a few moments he couldn't imagine breathing without her.

No, it wasn't real. A trick of his hormones. Or the tropical air.

It hadn't been real because who was he to be the judge of what was a real kiss or not? Georgia had told him she'd loved him and how had that turned out? He didn't know what was real. He didn't know the first thing about Summer's feelings, or even his own.

She was right: they had been pretending and had just been caught up in the act.

'It's been a fairly intense couple of days, don't you think?' she said.

'Definitely.'

'So, we just need to step back, take a break. Regroup?'

His thoughts exactly. 'Yes, I agree.' He could

have hugged her for being so understanding. But that would have got him into deeper trouble. He wasn't sure he'd be able to let her go next time.

Summer continued, 'And just to be clear, we agree this is a business arrangement. It's not real.' She was running her hands through her hair, the straps on her dress were askew and all he wanted at that moment was to scoop her up, take her to his room and relieve her of her dress and its wayward straps.

Instead, he lied, 'Of course it's not real.'

'Of course not, because we have a deal.'

'Rest assured—I don't do relationships.' It was difficult to speak, he was still out of breath. It felt like something was pressing heavily on his chest.

'So, a break? Regroup later?'

He nodded and Summer turned and fled to her room.

He was in serious, serious trouble. He'd messed up.

He took a deep breath and the panic lifted somewhat. No, it was okay. He just wouldn't do it again. He could control himself. Summer might be gorgeous and, yes, he admitted reluctantly, he was attracted to her. Very much.

But he could also stay professional.

He had to.

Will went to his own room and closed the door on the rest of the villa, and Summer. He just needed some time to himself. Time to breathe. He undressed and got into the shower, making the water as cold as he could get it. Which unfortunately, wasn't quite cold enough. His body still burned when he thought of kissing Summer. And as long as his body was this warm, he couldn't help but think of Summer.

He dressed in shorts and a T-shirt and lay on his bed with his phone. Summer had been right: he hadn't shared enough of himself with her. First, failing to tell her all about Georgia and now, not telling her much about Ben.

To be fair, he hardly spoke to anyone about Ben. That part of his life and those feelings had been tucked away somewhere. It was easier to just let them sit there and not deal with them. He was busy. He had important work to do and Ben didn't understand that.

But not only had he failed to share things with Summer, he hadn't got to know her as well as he should have. Ben and Gus had asked him questions today about Summer's music and he hadn't been able to answer them.

He looked up Summer on social media. It wasn't the first time; after making the deal with her he'd dutifully followed all her accounts. But this was the first time he'd actually thought to look up one of her songs. He realised his mistake. He should be familiar with her music; it was such a big part of *her* life.

Seeing Summer's beautiful face, he clicked on

one of her videos. She was sitting in an armchair in a room, in front of a wall covered in photographs, guitar on her lap. She looked down at her guitar and not at the camera, strumming gently, her fingers moving hypnotically over the strings.

The song was happy, sweet. It had been uploaded a year ago. When she was still with that jerk Michael. Will's chest constricted.

He hated that she'd felt this way about someone who'd hurt her.

He hated that she'd felt that way about someone who wasn't him.

Which was ridiculous, because he didn't even know Summer a year ago.

The latest songs were also sad. But also, angry. Raw. As you would be if your lover had taken your car and your grandfather's guitar. You'd be upset if someone stole an important part of your livelihood as well as an item of immense sentimental value.

Will lay on his bed, watching song after song. Captivated. Utterly addicted. Letting her beautiful voice wash over him and the lyrics swell his heart.

Doing absolutely nothing to cool him down.

Summer knocked firmly on Will's door. If he really did sleep naked then she didn't want to go barging in.

Or maybe she did. Though that would be wrong. And definitely not part of the deal.

'Will, you need to get up.'

Summer too would have been happy to go back to bed. What she'd experienced last night in her bedroom could not have been called sleep. Every time she'd felt herself drifting off, her body would recall the kiss she and Will had shared and jolt her alert and awake.

She'd never experienced a kiss like it. The way the world shifted when his lips were on hers, the way her bones seemed to melt under his touch. The desire began to rise in her again now but she batted it away. Again.

She knocked on his door again. 'We're meeting your mother for breakfast and we want to get out of here before she arrives on our doorstep and sees we slept in two beds last night.'

The door flew open before Summer could step out of the way and she was suddenly nose to nose with Will.

Both jumped back as though they had been jolted by an electric shock.

They arrived at the cafe to find Diane and Gus leaning close, foreheads touching over a menu. Will looked at Summer and she nodded. No matter what had happened between them last night, they had a job to do. He picked up her hand. They strode in together, hands clasped.

Diane looked up and smiled broadly. She stood and pulled her son into a hug. Will closed his eyes as he hugged her and something snagged in Summer's chest. Will was about a foot taller than his mother and their hug was full of affection.

She didn't want Diane to find out that her son had lied; she wanted everything to be okay between them. She wanted Will to be happy.

They sat, ordered breakfast, and then Gus asked, 'What are you two lovebirds doing today?'

'I have some work to do,' Will said, colour rising in his cheeks.

The older couple frowned. 'You're meant to be on holiday, you do remember that don't you? We have people covering for you back home. They know to call you when it is absolutely something you need to do yourself,' Diane said. Then she turned to Summer. 'He's not a good delegator.'

Summer nodded. 'A bit of a control freak.'

Diane laughed. 'Isn't he just?'

Summer's chest warmed. She didn't always understand him, but she was definitely getting to know him. Summer picked up Will's hand. He squeezed hers. An invisible force was pushing them together. Like an addiction. If her hand was not in his there was something missing.

Except that it's not real. It's only an act.

'You should go kayaking. Or surfing. Do you surf, Summer?' Gus asked.

'Not often,' Summer said.

'Really? Will loves to.'

'I know,' she said and leaned into him.

He smiled back at her. 'She prefers to watch me,' he said with a glint in his eye.

Summer laughed and her face went red. She'd never seen him surf, but suspected he was right; the view of Will on a surfboard would be something worth watching.

She leant over and kissed his cheek. It was daring, but felt right. It felt like something a flirty couple would do, and was that what they were meant to be? It was so easy to kiss him. And as long as they were physically affectionate with one another they were convincing as a couple.

'Oh, I know I've said it before, but it's so lovely to see you both together.' Diane's face was so earnest, Summer had to look away.

'Summer, I have a favour to ask. Will you help me get ready before my wedding? I won't keep you long from Will, but I need someone to pick up my flowers just before the ceremony and to zip me into my dress. And I'd love it if you would.'

Summer's stomach dropped. It was an honour… but…she looked up at Will. His face was frozen. She had to say yes, she couldn't not, but she could taste the bitterness of the lie on her tongue.

'I don't have a daughter and I'm not sure that Will or Ben want to help their mother into her dress.'

'I'd love to. It would be an honour.'

Diane exhaled. 'Thank you, the honour is all mine.'

Summer looked at Will and the pair exchanged forced smiles.

'So, surfing? Kayaking? What's it to be?' Gus said. 'Summer, you have to get this man to take a break.'

Summer was relieved to get back to the villa. This was their safe space, the place they could be themselves, with no need to pretend.

Will went to his room, no doubt to sneak in some work phone calls and Summer took her notebook out to the deck to work on some lyrics. She wrote down a few lines, even hummed a tune or two but longed for her guitar.

That's what this is all about, remember? In a few days you'll be home and you will have your guitar back. The thought sustained her, even as the only lyrics she could come up with were ones about first kisses. Longing. Forbidden desire.

She sighed.

'Hey,' Will said a while later, jolting her from her fantasy of kissing him in the pool. 'What are you up to?'

'Just making some notes. Thinking about a new song.'

'Great,' he said. 'Your songs are good.'

'How have you heard my songs?'

He held up his phone. 'Online. I looked you up.'

'Oh.'

'What kind of boyfriend would I be if I didn't know your songs?'

She nodded. She'd looked him up as well, but she still felt exposed that he'd listened to any of her old songs. Especially the ones about Michael, both the happy and the sad.

'They're really good. I didn't realise that you wrote that song for Ash Cooper.'

Cooper had been the biggest artist in the country a decade ago and the song she'd written had been one of his biggest hits.

'Yeah, well.' Summer pulled her knees up to her chest.

'That song was huge. You must still be earning royalties from it.'

She buried her face in her knees. She didn't want to hear this. Not from him, of all people. Not from Mr Carefully Drafted Contract. He'd know once and for all that she was a flake.

'What's the matter?' he asked.

'I signed away my rights to it.'

'What do you mean?'

'The copyright, all future royalties.'

'You got nothing?'

'They paid me one thousand dollars at the time. It was so much money and I didn't get anyone to look over the contract. I was so excited that he wanted to sing my song.'

'Oh, Summer.'

It was bad enough hearing the pity in his voice,

she couldn't bear to see it on his handsome face as well. She pressed her face into her palms.

'Yes, I know, I should've been more careful. I should've got a lawyer. But I trusted him. I trusted them all. And I was so excited.'

Will didn't respond and she didn't look up, but eventually she felt the cushion next to her sag with his weight. He placed a hand gently on her shoulder. It didn't feel like pity, it felt like understanding.

'I'm so sorry.'

She lifted her head. 'I know—I don't even want to think about what might have been. How my life might have been different, so please don't try and tell me. I know it was a monumental mistake to not get someone to look carefully at the contract. Just like all the other mistakes I've made in my life.'

'We all make mistakes.'

'Yeah, I bet you never signed a contract so disadvantageous to you.'

He sighed. 'I've trusted the wrong people too.'

Georgia. He wasn't going to open her wound and she would do the same courtesy.

He'd trusted Georgia and been let down, just like she'd trusted Michael.

'It's a great song, Summer. And so are your others.'

Their gazes locked and her cheeks warmed. She was about to lean in and thought he was too.

Until now, *magnetism* has just been a word. But now she understood the cliché. When her hand wasn't on his arm, she was being pulled towards him, their bodies locked together.

No.

It was an act and it was confusing her.

The aim for this week was to convince Will's family they could be a couple, not to convince herself. The last thing she needed was to leave Bali with a crush on Will. That would be excess baggage she could not afford.

She got up. 'I just remembered I need to call my mum,' she said and went to her room.

Summer chatted with Penny for a while and then lay down. She read for a while but must have drifted off to sleep. When she woke, the sky was darkening and her stomach rumbled.

She opened her door and walked out onto the deck. Will was sitting on one of the daybeds, hunched over his phone.

'Are you still working?'

He turned to her and put his phone down, but not his tension. Will was coiled so tightly her own shoulders ached.

'Will, you seriously need to stop for a moment. Look at where you are.'

Will glanced towards the ocean then looked down again.

'Can you look me in the eyes and tell me you see a view as beautiful as this every day?'

Summer walked towards him and stood behind him. His square shoulders were magnificent but so tight. She reached down and lay her palms on them and squeezed. When he didn't react, she began to press and kneed, to search out the knots and massage them away. She wrapped her fingers around the front side of his shoulders, to the muscles below his collarbone and rubbed them as well, dragging her thumbs over the muscles in his back. He moaned and she froze. She should have asked first, shouldn't have just gone straight in, and started rubbing him.

He froze when she did.

'Sorry, that was presumptuous of me,' she said but didn't lift her hands.

'Don't stop. Unless you want to.'

She kept going. His flesh under hers felt so good, tight, but firm and strong. She could feel the tension ebbing away as she rubbed him.

'Summer, that feels so good.' His voice was almost a whimper. She wanted to lift his shirt and find the muscles lower down his back. Lower down his front. She settled with gently rubbing his neck, even going so far as to slip her fingertips into his hairline, touching his thick, soft hair.

Will turned and their gazes met, his eyelids heavy with want. He moved a hand up around her waist and pulled Summer onto his lap.

Every breath left her body and the air, already heavy with the afternoon humidity, weighed even heavier on them. It would be so simple to bridge those last inches to his lips, fall into this, let go once and for all. Will's arm slid up her back and into her hair too. She felt her body sway. She felt everything sway.

'At what point do we accept that there is something real here?' she asked.

'There can't be. I'm paying you.'

'I know. We agreed.'

Confusion creased his brow. 'We wouldn't be lying to them any more if this was real,' he reasoned.

She shook her head. No. That didn't make sense. They'd still be lying. Only the lie would be messier and harder to keep straight.

'We would. And it'd be harder to remember where the lie begins and where it ends.'

Will nodded; he leant forward but just rested his forehead on hers. He sighed.

'You and I...for real. It's impossible. We both know that,' she said.

'Why? Remind me again, because right now it feels so right.' He pulled back and smiled at her.

She smiled back.

'You're a billionaire, I'm a busker. You don't do relationships—you don't trust anyone. I just got my heart broken. Remember?'

He shook his head. 'Trivial details,' he said, but she knew he was joking.

With all her willpower, Summer pulled herself up and off his lap.

'Let's go out and get some dinner together. And then maybe watch a movie. Let's celebrate the fact that after today we only have two full days to get through.'

Will nodded. The wedding was the day after tomorrow and they were getting to the end of all the family obligations Will had. They couldn't relax, exactly, but there was every reason to think that they would successfully keep Will's lie a secret.

'It sounds like a plan, Summer Bright.'

At what point do we accept there's something real here?

Never, was his initial thought. Because there wasn't, there couldn't be. Yet she'd been sitting on his lap and he'd been seconds away from kissing her, hours after he'd sworn never to again.

They enjoyed a nice meal out and watched a movie together, talking for the third night in a row into the early hours. He enjoyed her company. They didn't have to spend so much time together when the others weren't around, but Will found himself enjoying the time he spent alone with Summer far more than the time he spent with his family. It wasn't just that the pressure to perform wasn't there, it was that Summer was becoming his friend. His confidant. She listened to him, without judgement and he was finding that it was natural to open up to her.

And he wanted to know all about her. Their lives were different, but that wasn't a barrier to friendship, he realised. She'd had so many experiences he couldn't have dreamt of: going on the road with the tribute shows, busking in central Adelaide, various odd jobs over the years, encounters with all sorts of people in the music industry. Her life had been fun, filled with laughter and happy applause from her audiences. He recalled from the night of the charity gala how much fun the audience had had. Summer brought joy to people's lives and he was in awe of that.

The next morning, as usual, Summer was up before him. She was sitting on the deck in a broad-brimmed hat and cute floral sundress.

I'm going to miss this.

He shook his head.

No, he wouldn't. It was going be a relief to get home and put this behind him. It would be a relief to stop lying.

She beamed when he sat down next to her.

'Morning. How did you sleep?'

'Like a log. You?' It was a white lie, like every other night they had been here he'd found it impossible to relax enough to sleep and thoughts of Summer kept sneaking back into his thoughts. And last night, into his dreams.

'Great. What's on the schedule today?'

'Nothing scheduled. I've told Mum I'll see her at some stage, but you don't have to come.'

'I'd be happy to. She might think it's strange if I'm not with you.'

He nodded. He had to focus on why she was here. Their charade had been working so far—it would be a shame to ruin it now.

Will checked his emails and Summer lay by the pool reading her book. He looked at her, jealously.

Working had never bothered him before. He'd enjoyed it; it gave him strength. It gave his life meaning.

You're on holiday.

Maybe his mother was right—he needed to remember he was on holiday. And maybe Summer was right as well. Did he use work as a distraction? Did he use work as an excuse not to have a life?

'Do you want to go surfing?'

Summer looked up from her book and her mouth dropped. 'Do you?'

'Yes, this is ridiculous—we've been here for four days and we haven't gone.'

'I haven't done it for ages.'

'You won't forget how.'

She laughed. 'Maybe not, but I'm not as young as I once was.'

Will looked at her. Summer had gorgeous curves, but her legs were lean and strong. 'You look pretty fit to me.'

Her face reddened. He'd meant to allay her fears, but maybe he had crossed a line. But Summer was attractive. And fit and surely, she knew that? 'Let's go then. Now.' Suddenly there was nothing he wanted to do more. How long had it been? Ages. He'd been so caught up at work. He swam most mornings, but that was just in the pool at the bottom of his building and it had been too long since he'd felt the salt water of the ocean on his skin.

'Don't you have to work?'

'I am meant to be on holiday. I thought you'd think it was a good idea if I relaxed?'

She laughed. 'It would be. Let's do it.'

They passed Ben and Charlotte on their way to the beach.

'Hey, having a good day?' Summer asked them.

'Great,' Ben and Charlotte replied at once.

'We're just off to the beach. Do you want to join us?' Will asked. He didn't overthink it; his brother was here. Ben and Charlotte looked at one another and then nodded in unison. 'Yes,' they said.

'Great.' Will was with his brother for the first time in years; they should spend some time together, bridge the gulf between them. It wasn't too late.

Will was partly relieved, partly disappointed to see that Summer wore a long rashie over her swimsuit to protect her from the sun. It was probably sensible; her skin was pale and no doubt sensitive to too much sun. But it didn't stop him furtively admiring her curves and wishing for the hundredth time that day that they had met under different circumstances and he hadn't signed an ironclad agreement not to have a physical relationship with her. Or that he hadn't lied to his mother and his board about being in a relationship with her.

Yes, there were all kinds of reasons why they shouldn't have a physical relationship, but somehow, when he was around her, none of those reasons seemed to be very important.

They hired surfboards and Will made sure Summer remembered the basics.

When Ben and Charlotte arrived, Will and Ben took Summer out to the waves, the surf break being a decent paddle from the beach itself.

Ben hadn't been surfing for even longer than Will and the brothers naturally made fun of one another's rustiness, making Summer laugh. Ben also helped give Summer some pointers, and they all enjoyed the crystal-clear waters. The bobbing of the swell was calming and invigorating, Will scarcely wanted to get out of the ocean. This was such a good plan; they should have been doing this every afternoon.

Will, who hadn't been as sensible as Summer by wearing a rashie felt the skin on his shoulders start to tighten, a sure sign he needed to reapply sunscreen. He left Ben and Summer waiting for the next wave and paddled back into shore. After reapplying sun protection, he couldn't help himself but took his phone out to see how the markets had closed in Australia. Then, seeing that Ben and Summer were getting along so well he turned and made a quick phone call.

Will heard Charlotte gasp loudly. Then swear.

With his back to the ocean, he didn't see what she had seen, but when he swung back around all he could see was white foam and no sign of either Ben. Or Summer.

CHAPTER NINE

WILL DROPPED HIS phone and ran to the water. Lifeguards were also gathering and jet skis were being dragged to the water's edge. But there had been several dozen people out when the freak wave had hit. There were not many lifeguards.

Will strode into the water, but the swell was still too high, too choppy for him to be able to make out anything or anyone. Besides, the break was about fifty metres from the shore. Was he going to swim it? Or get his board?

He turned and went for his board, judging that he'd make up the time once he was back in the water. Once he had retrieved it and was heading back into the surf a lifeguard waved him back, but Will pretended not to understand, taking long strokes, and trying to battle his way toward the spot he'd last seen his brother and Summer.

A small dingy and some jet skis passed Will and he envied their speed as he headed slowly out towards the break, feeling sicker and sicker with each stroke.

Will soon realised how pointless it was, he

couldn't see either Ben or Summer and the break was still so far away. How could he possibly find them?

Finally, one of the boats headed back, passed him and pointed to the beach. Will knew it was hopeless, with his chest burning he turned and swam back to the shore, panic rising even further with each stroke. By the time he reached the beach, exhausted and with his heart racing he was more terrified than he'd ever been in his life.

Please make her okay...please let her be fine.

He made so many deals with heaven he knew he'd never be able to repay all the promises he'd made to the universe at the moment. There was a lifeless body on the beach, the size and shape of Summer. He collapsed on the sand next to her, seeing for the first time that she was moving and coughing up water. He took her hand, not caring for a second what she was coughing up on him.

'It's going to be okay,' he whispered, as much to her as to himself.

When she had recovered enough to turn and focus on him, he pulled her into his arms and hugged her.

Summer hurt in about one million places. And a million more she didn't even know existed in her body. Her throat throbbed. Her eyes stung from all the salt water. Her leg hurt from where the surfboard had tugged and eventually broken free.

And her right shoulder pounded for some reason she had absolutely no recollection of.

The whole incident was a blur. She remembered watching Ben, waiting for his next instruction, and then the sky had gone dark, like a cloud was passing across the sun. By the time she realised it was a wave, it was already on top of her, and there was barely enough time to take a breath, let alone brace herself.

The water had tossed her around and around until she didn't know which way was up. She'd scrambled in what she'd thought was the right direction, but couldn't reach air or even sand to be able to tell. Each time she thought she might be making progress the water would toss her in the other direction, and then nothing.

It was Will she saw first. She was on the beach, throat stinging from coughing up half the ocean, her chest aching. She may have even vomited. Maybe even on Will. She wasn't sure. It was a while before she could open her eyes and actually focus and when she did, it was only one face she saw amongst all the others. He was sitting next to her, holding her hand. The second thing she noticed was the look in his eyes. It was terror.

For a second she thought, *Oh, my goodness, Ben. Something's happened to Ben.*

But then she realised Ben was also sitting next to her and watching with concern.

You. He's worried about you.

* * *

Summer was seen to by two paramedics who checked her over and asked her questions. Yes, she knew what year it was. It was a Friday. She was in Nusa Lembongan. And yes, she was okay, though when she tried to stand her knees gave way.

'I just want to rest. I'm fine,' she kept saying. And she felt that she was, just wiped out. Battered. But intact.

She lay back down on the sand, resting while everyone around her talked in various languages. She could just sleep there.

After a while, maybe minutes, maybe even seconds, Will shook her gently and said, 'We're going to take you to the medical centre to get you looked at. Can you sit? Do you think you can stand?'

At the clinic they gave her some paracetamol and anti-inflammatories and told Will to call immediately if her condition changed. Summer thought she understood everything well enough, but she felt that she could trust Will completely to remember all the instructions they gave him about medication and what to do. Summer let herself be led out of the medical centre and into a waiting taxi truck.

Diane was waiting for them back at the villa, pacing outside, but rushed over when she saw them. Will held one side of her and Diane took the other. Summer wanted to tell them both that she was fine and could walk by herself, but she let them lead her inside.

They sat her on the sofa, but what she really wanted to do was lie down.

At the medical centre, the nurse had helped her out of her swimming suit and into the sundress she'd worn over but she was suddenly conscious that she wasn't actually wearing any underwear under it.

'I'd like to get changed,' she said.

'Of course,' Diane said. 'Go help her,' she ordered Will.

Too exhausted to make an excuse for him, Summer let him lead her to her bedroom. The more time that passed, the easier it was to walk on her own, but she let herself be led into her room and to her bed.

Will closed her bedroom door and looked around. 'What do you want to wear?'

'PJs?'

'Good idea.'

He went to her suitcase, but she reached under her pillow to where she'd placed hers that morning and grinned at him.

'You can leave me, you know.'

Will grimaced, clearly torn. 'I can't really, you know. I need to keep an eye on you. I'll turn around.' Which he dutifully did.

'I'm not sure how that's helping,' she replied, but was also too sore to argue much. She tugged at her dress, but her shoulder snagged and she groaned. Will spun around and rushed to her. 'What is it?'

'It's just my shoulder. It hurts to lift my arm.'

She wanted to get out of the dress, it was damp and sandy and itched her already aching body even more. If she was really being honest with herself, she really wanted a shower as well. She wanted a shower more than she wanted to hide her naked body from Will. 'I'll tell you what—if you promise to keep your eyes half-closed and instantly forget everything you see, you can help me.'

'I promise.'

'I think I want a shower though.'

'Okay, come with me.'

Summer almost laughed at Will's businesslike approach.

In the bathroom he started the shower then turned back to Summer. 'I'll close my eyes,' he promised.

'That could be worse—you'll have to feel your way.' She giggled.

He didn't laugh but his face reddened. He took the hem of her dress and then shut his eyes, keeping them closed as he lifted the dress over her head. It was loose, but she still felt a stab of pain as he pulled it over her head. She was grateful for the pain though as it stopped her from thinking about the fact that Will could at this very second be looking at her naked torso.

The shower was separated from the bathroom by a screen so she was out of his view, though he was still in the room. And she was glad of that. She didn't want to be alone. She let the warm water wash over her and through her hair, washing away the salt and whatever else the ordeal had left on her.

She turned off the water and reached for a towel, left in easy reach. She managed to dry herself effectively, even with her sore shoulder. The nurse had assured her it was probably just a soft tissue injury and would settle in a day or two. She wrapped the towel around herself and emerged.

'Okay?' Will asked.

'Yes. Much better.'

Back at her bed, she pulled her pyjama pants on under the towel without too much trouble, but knew that getting the top over her head would be the challenge. She picked up the top and tried to lift it over her head.

Will pounced. 'Let me. I won't look.'

Summer didn't feel shy or even concerned that Will had any motive other than helping her. She trusted him. And she was totally comfortable. She stood.

He helped her manoeuvre her right arm into the armhole first and Summer managed the left. Then she let the towel drop and let Will help her get her head through the hole. The whole thing took less than ten seconds and when it was over, she felt like a new person, clean and mostly dry.

Her long thick hair was still wet and in the absence of drying it, she would usually pull it into a loose braid. She lifted her arm to do so, but again her shoulder snagged.

'What is it?'

'My hair.'

'What can I do?'

'You expect me to believe you're an expert in women's hairstyles?'

'I have many talents.' He smiled at her and something bloomed in her chest.

'Including hair?'

'No, not at all.' He smiled.

She laughed. 'Do you think you could help me with a basic braid, that will keep it out of my face?'

'I can try.'

She found her brush and a hair tie and sat with her back to Will. He was so gentle, so afraid of hurting her she had to reassure him that he could tug harder. As she sat there, with Will gently brushing and drying her hair she felt herself relax and all the worries of the past few hours began to slip away. After a while he presented her with a neat, perfectly suitable plait.

If he ever has daughters he will be able to take on hair duty, she thought. The image of a dark-haired little girl, with long curly locks and

Will's beautiful eyes jumped into her mind. She squashed it away with a hint of pain. It wouldn't be her daughter whose hair he brushed and braided.

'You should lie down now. I'll get rid of Mum.'

Summer followed Will out of her room, doubtful Diane would leave without checking for herself that Summer was okay.

Seeing her freshly washed and ready for a rest, Diane moved in for a hug.

'I'm so glad you're fine. What a relief. Get some rest,' she said to Summer. She turned to Will, 'Look after her. Don't take your eyes off her.'

Diane kissed her lightly on the cheek and Summer went back to her bed.

'She's fine. I'll look after her,' she heard Will say.

'Of course. But let me know if there's anything I can do. Shall I come over with some dinner later?'

'Mum, it's the night before your wedding. You're meant to be having dinner with Gus's parent's, aren't you? We'll be fine.'

After seeing his mother off, Will came back to her room, but this time he waited at the door.

'You need to rest, but I don't want to leave you on your own.'

Summer imagined him stepping away from the door, going to his own room and didn't like the feeling that came over her. She patted the bed next to her.

'I could sit on the armchair.'

'I'd like you next to me.'

Will walked slowly into the room. 'Are you all right?'

'Yes, I'm fine. But I don't want to be alone.' The adrenaline and all the chemicals that had kept her going since the wave were wearing off; she was exhausted but also now left with the feeling of what a close shave she'd had. How lucky she'd been. But as long as Will was next to her she felt calmer. Secure. 'Can you stay here, please? Hold me?'

Without another word Will joined her on the bed. She lay on her side, facing away from him and he lay behind her, pulling her into a hug. She instantly felt better. Lying in Will's arms she knew everything would be okay.

Summer woke when the sun was low in the sky. She still ached, but her head was clear. She was in her bed, no longer being embraced, but could sense Will was still beside her.

She rolled over.

Will was next to her, propped up on some pillows and looking at his phone. He put it down when she turned.

'Hey, how are you feeling?'

Summer stretched, assessed her body. 'Not worse. My head feels better. I feel a bit fragile, but okay. Thanks for staying here with me.'

'Of course.'

'I don't know quite what came over me before.'

'Shock, probably.'

Yes, shock. That was it. Nothing more, or less. She'd needed his embrace.

She still needed it.

'I'm so sorry,' he said.

'What for?'

'I said I'd teach you.'

'And you did.'

'But I wasn't watching—I wasn't paying attention. I was working.'

'You went to get sunscreen!'

'But then I stayed and made a phone call. And that happened.'

Will blamed himself, but that was ridiculous.

'Ben was there.'

'I should have been there.'

Will's jaw was tight and his eyes hard. But she understood now that his aloofness, this barrier he kept against the world wasn't malicious, it was to protect him. She touched his arm gently. When he didn't flinch, she spread her fingers over his forearm and held it. 'I'm okay, everything's okay.'

Under her touch she felt his muscles soften. But just a little.

'I thought…for a moment… I thought you were dead.'

'But I'm not. I'm here.'

Hold me, she wanted to say again. *And never let me go.*

But Will seemed oblivious to her touch, still tortured by what had happened at the beach.

It was easier for her, in a way. She'd been knocked unconscious almost immediately and when she'd woken, she'd been on the beach, breathing. She thought of how she would have felt if their positions had been reversed. For Will, watching powerless from the beach, it would have been awful. Especially as control was something he clung to like a security blanket.

'You can't blame yourself—this sort of thing could have happened to anyone. It could have happened with you right there. You would've been wiped out too.'

'But I would've been watching.'

'Will, please, you've looked after me. You've been wonderful. Please stop worrying. I'm going to be okay.'

'Is there anything you need? Do you want to call your mother?'

Summer shook her head. 'No, I'll tell her all about it when I get back. For now, she'd only worry. What I do want though, is something to eat. I don't even remember if we had lunch.'

Thankfully Will smiled. This was something he could control. 'What do you feel like? Curry? Noodles? Or something entirely different? I'll get anything you want.'

* * *

Despite what Summer had said, it was his fault. He should have been in the water with her. Not checking his emails. If he'd been closer, if he'd been paying attention, then they all might have been prepared for the wave and managed to ride it out. He wasn't sure how. Ducking under. Bracing themselves better. But he'd have been there, closer. He couldn't shake the feeling that he should have done more.

Sitting next to him now, after dinner, she seemed fine. But Will wasn't sure if he was. They were sitting together on the couch, watching a movie, and resting. Summer was enjoying herself, laughing and sighing at the appropriate parts, but Will was having trouble following the plot.

It all turned out okay. Summer is fine, sitting here with you now.

But it almost hadn't. Summer was seconds, inches from being seriously hurt. Or worse. He knew, from watching his father pass away, that the difference between life and death was so fragile, so thin.

The thought of something happening to Summer made his gut tighten. Every time he thought of the white waves curdling the sea she and Ben had been stuck in he wanted to be sick.

His mother and brother had both called to check in on Summer and him, but otherwise they had had a quiet evening.

Summer yawned. 'I think I'm going to call it a night.'

'Good idea. Will you be okay?'

'I think so. But…'

Will froze. 'What?'

'But if you wanted to sit with me for a bit, that would be all right.'

'Are you sure you're all right?'

'For the hundredth time, yes. But it's been a big day and I don't want to be alone.'

'I don't want you to be alone. I'd feel better if I was with you.'

Summer reached over and squeezed his hand. 'I know that too.' And then she released it, but that touch alone reached something deep inside him he wasn't even sure he'd noticed before.

He'd come to care about her in the past few days. It wasn't part of the plan. It didn't even make sense, but there was no other way of explaining how shaken he'd been following the wave.

She's become your friend.

Yes, that was it. Friends.

As he stretched out on the bed next to her he felt himself relax. As long as he was here next to her everything was all right.

The last thing he wanted to do was undress her and kiss her all over. Part of him still wanted to do that, but the bigger part just wanted this. To lie next to her, to hear her breathing and to know that she was okay.

CHAPTER TEN

THE SUN STREAKING in at the edges of the closed blinds woke Summer gently. She lay there for a while, letting the events of the day before coming back to her gradually and taking in her current surroundings. She was in her room in a comfortable bed, but she wasn't alone.

Will lay next to her, facing her, his arm on her shoulder, but that was the only place they were touching. She could hear him breathing with the intensity of someone in a deep sleep. *I wonder if he's wearing anything*, she thought, and almost giggled, but didn't want to in case she woke him.

She was sore and stiff, but she wasn't in any pain, weirdly most of the soreness settled around her neck and shoulders, similar to a whiplash she'd once experienced after a rear-end collision. Her throat was a little scratchy, but all in all she thought she felt fine in herself.

Her last recollection from the night before was her lying on her bed and Will sitting up next to her reading to her. She'd insisted that she was fine and he'd insisted that he'd just stay until she was asleep. He must've fallen asleep himself.

Summer needed to use the bathroom and she was going to have to wake him eventually. She moved gently towards her side of the bed and his hand fell. She turned back to look at him sleeping.

How was this man so beautiful? And so full of surprises. A week ago, she could never have guessed that they would have spent the night sleeping next to one another, even platonically. She never would have guessed how peaceful Mr Excel Spreadsheet would look in his sleep. Will's eyelashes flickered and his eyes began to open. She knew she should leave and not be caught watching him, but she couldn't help it. She stared and waited for the moment his eyes began to focus, and then he would see her. Still drowsy from sleep, and totally unguarded. At that instant, he smiled and Summer's heart turned to a puddle.

'Hey, sleepyhead,' she said.

'Hey,' he answered.

'Despite the rumours, you do sleep in clothes. I have to say I'm a little disappointed.'

She knew she shouldn't flirt with him like this, but just as with everything else when it came to Will, she couldn't help herself.

'How are you feeling?' he rubbed his head and with his hair sticking up he looked even more adorable. She liked when he looked scruffy.

'I'm okay, really. A little stiff, but I think after a shower I'll be good.'

'You're taking it easy today.'

'It's the wedding! The whole reason I came.'

'Relax, we'll go to the wedding, but apart from that I think you should take it easy here.' Will stretched his arms high and closed his eyes as he did it, and she sneaked a further look at his T-shirt, riding up and exposing his taut, flat stomach.

Damn clause six.

'Hop in the shower,' he said. 'Breakfast should be here soon.'

'I'm supposed to go and help your mother get ready, remember?' Summer hadn't forgotten. Diane's comment that she didn't have a daughter stuck in Summer's gut and made her feel worse about the lie she and Will were telling. Diane had asked her to help her get ready for the wedding under false pretences. She wasn't Will's girlfriend, she wasn't about to be Diane's daughter-in-law, she had no business helping her get ready for her wedding.

'She'll understand. She'll want you to rest. Charlotte can help her.'

Summer didn't want to let Diane down, but was also grateful to have one less opportunity to slip up. 'Okay.'

'In fact, you should have a bath.'

Summer rarely had baths—there wasn't one in

her apartment so they felt like such an extravagance.

A few hours later after a long bath, a leisurely breakfast, and a stretch by the pool, Summer went to put on the dress she was going to wear to the wedding.

It was another purchase from the op shop. One of the main advantages of working there, apart from the casual hours, was that she got first claim at new merchandise. She hadn't had a chance to wear this particular find, something originally from the nineteen-eighties, but by a well-known designer. It had likely been sitting at the back of a closet for thirty years by the time it made its way to the op shop in near perfect condition. A bluish-green colour that made her eyes look even more intense.

When she emerged from the bedroom and Will turned to look, he pulled a face.

'What's the matter? Is it not good enough?'

He shook his head. 'It's a beautiful dress. I've just never seen you in that colour. It looks amazing with your eyes.'

'Thank you.' Summer dropped her head and couldn't look at him. If he liked it, why had he frowned?

'You look beautiful, beautiful, Summer.'

Chairs were set out on the beach, decorated with green leaves and the bright orange and red of tropical blooms. A circle of flowers lay before the chairs, where the celebrant stood, waiting. Brightly coloured umbrellas stood around, providing partial shade. Some of the guests held pretty parasols to keep the sun away.

Will stood to the left of the celebrant, and next to Ben. He wore long pants and a white shirt, open at the collar and with the sleeves rolled up. Summer sat near the front and while she tried to focus on the happy couple and their vows her eyes kept darting back to Will.

As soon as the ceremony was over, Will was back by her side and holding her hand. It didn't feel like they were pretending any longer; it just felt right. Everyone was in a celebratory mood. Having had the chance to get to know one another over the past five or six days Summer felt like she'd come to know everyone so well. With a twinge she realised that this was nearly it, this was their last night and she'd say goodbye to everyone tonight or tomorrow.

She was having such a lovely time she'd begun to forget that she wasn't really a guest, wasn't a part of this family. And never would be. She and Will might have acknowledged that they were attracted to one another, but they had also spoken about why anything more than a flirtation would be impossible between them.

She didn't belong in his world and his made no sense to her. Here, away from real life, things were deceptively simple, but back in Adelaide, he'd be working away in his skyscraper and she'd be dragging her guitar over the city. She'd be scraping together each dollar she earned and he'd be putting together million-dollar deals, not even worrying if he could afford a cup of coffee.

It would be especially sad to say goodbye to Charlotte, which was silly as they hadn't even known one another a week, but she'd become such a part of Summer's life.

'I can't believe this is it!' Charlotte said, echoing Summer's thoughts. 'This is our last night,'

'Ours too,' Summer said.

'I'm so looking forward to you and Will coming to London.'

Summer smiled and let herself imagine for just a moment visiting London, a city she'd never been to, with Will. Seeing some sights, hanging out with Charlotte and Ben in some of the supercool places they no doubt frequented.

Just being anywhere with Will would be lovely...

No. She shook the fantasy away.

'I need photos,' Charlotte declared.

The women took some selfies together, then Charlotte said, 'And now some of you, you gorgeous pair.'

Summer and Will scooted closer and after a blink of approval from Summer, Will slid his arm around her waist and pulled her to him. Melting into Will's embrace it was easy to smile. Summer wasn't acting at all.

Charlotte gave a gooey smile. 'Look, see?' Charlotte held out the phone to them. 'You two are adorable.'

She looked at the photo, a close-up of their faces, their cheeks almost touching. She could still feel his body pressed against hers. Both pairs of eyes were smiling at the camera. His brilliant blue, hers deep, mossy green. Together they made aquamarine.

Will looked around the beach as the crowd thinned out. The day had gone well, mostly because Summer had been at his side almost all of the time. She was glowing in the fading light and her beautiful dress, so far from the barely breathing woman he'd sat with on the beach yesterday, but he still kept reaching over to take her hand, or touch her arm or to simply look at her, to reassure himself that everything was fine.

Before they'd left Adelaide, Will had offered to say some words at the reception after the wedding. While Diane could speak for herself, and did, at length, Will felt that someone from her family should also say something. Her father had passed away, and then of course, her first husband.

Will had prepared some words a week ago but as he read them over now, he knew they were not quite right. He kept the shell of the speech, thanking everyone for coming, welcoming Gus to their family, but his first speech hadn't mentioned anything about what had brought Gus and his mother together in the first place.

It was a glaring omission. Just as important as all the other things.

'Mum, Gus, you two are an inspiration. You've reminded us about second chances and the power of love to heal. You've shown us that it is possible to love again after heartbreak.

'By taking these vows today, in front of all of us, you've shown how important love is. You both know what it is to lose love, and yet you love anyway. Bravely and with purpose.'

His eyes started to fill. This was love. He was witnessing it; unconventional, unexplainable. But unmistakable. His chest was full as he walked back to Summer. When she saw his glassy eyes, she smiled, slid her soft arms around his waist and pulled him close. His heart swelled even further; he thought it would burst.

'Thank you,' he whispered.

'What for?'

'For everything. For coming.'

'I'm glad I did.'

'Really? I've put you through hell. And I nearly got you killed.'

'It's been an adventure.'

He laughed. That's what he loved about Summer, her ability to put a positive spin on almost everything.

Love? No, it was what he admired about Summer. What he *liked* about Summer.

And he did like her, there was no point denying that. He liked her a lot.

The remarkable thing was that for most of the day he'd stopped worrying about the lies they were meant to be telling. He was with Summer. And he didn't care who believed it or not. They were friends, she was with him.

It stopped being an act and was simply fact. They might not have been an actual couple, together for two years, but they were a type of couple. Unconventional, to be sure, but that didn't mean they didn't have a bond, a common purpose.

He trusted her. They were a team.

After Diane and Gus had made their goodbyes, Will looked to Summer and she nodded. She'd had a long day and he wasn't going to make it any longer by lingering until every guest had left.

He went to order a taxi, but she waved him away.

'I'm fine to walk. It isn't far.'

They bid everyone else a goodnight and hugged them all. There were tentative plans for everyone to share a post-wedding breakfast before everyone flew home, but Will had the feeling that he and Summer had done what they needed to. It was over.

They walked slowly along the footpath the short distance to their villa. The sky was dark, but the air filled with the sound of singing cicadas. He wanted to stop right there and pull her into his arms. Feel her body against his, taste her lips on his.

You made a deal. You agreed that you wouldn't have a physical relationship. That was why Summer agreed to come here with you.

He couldn't renege on that arrangement now. That would mean going back on his word and he didn't do that, as a businessman or a man. If everyone went around backing out of deals, breaking promises, then no one could trust anyone.

But what if the deal was over? What if it was done? What then?

'We've got through the wedding, but what happens next? Back in Adelaide?' Will asked.

'We break up. Wasn't that the plan?'

'Yes, of course,' he said. He wasn't sure why he'd asked the question.

But was it the plan? What if the agreement was just to come with him to the wedding. Now the wedding was over, could he trust her with a new sort of deal? One that definitely did not involve a clause six.

Back at the villa, Summer flopped onto the couch by the pool and slipped off her shoes. She was exhausted, but also exhilarated. They'd done it. They'd made it through the wedding and no one had doubted—at least not seriously—that she and Will were a couple.

In about twenty-four hours they would be on a plane back home and it would all be over. Summer's phone pinged and she picked it up. Someone had paid seven thousand, seven hundred dollars into her account.

It could only be one person.

'You paid me. Already. Why?'

Will sat down next to her on the couch. 'The wedding's over. You've fulfilled your end of the bargain.'

'But we're not home yet.'

'I want it to be over.' Will's eyes were serious and his voice low.

'You want me to leave? Now?' Her heart cracked, but she went to stand.

He placed a hand gently on her arm. 'No, I want the deal to be over. I don't want the money to be between us any more. I want to rip clause six to shreds.'

Understanding his meaning, and without saying anything further, Summer stood and went to her room. She reached into her bag and pulled out the contract.

'What are you doing?'

She picked up one of the lamps containing lit candles that adorned the deck, lifted the protective glass, and touched the paper to the flame.

They both watched, mesmerised as the flames

licked the paper, curling gently around it, erasing the deal they had signed. But suddenly the flames took off, engulfing the pages and her fingertips. She cried, 'Blast!' and dropped the paper. 'It was supposed to be more elegant than that.'

Will stepped on the paper with his shoe, extinguishing the flames, a smile creeping over his face.

'I don't know, I thought it was pretty great.' Will stepped towards her and Summer held her breath. 'Just like you.'

He reached for her chin, held her face like it was the most precious thing in the world and tilted her mouth to his.

This kiss was like none of the others, there was nothing to hold them back, they were doing this simply because they wanted to, nothing more. Or less.

Gently at first, his lips teased hers with their softness. But Summer had waited too long. She opened her mouth, welcoming him, letting him know that she understood him and that she wanted this as much as he did. She threw her arms around him, wanting all of him and as soon as possible.

Tonight, they were equals, here because they both wanted to be. For tonight, at least, there was nothing between them. Except their clothes, which Summer started to deal with as quickly as possible. Her fingers deftly unbuttoned Will's shirt and, in a rush of relief she slid her hands into his shirt, over his bare chest and back. One of the many things she'd been dreaming of doing all week. Will's torso was simply spectacular, hard, smooth and the perfect fit for her hands to slide over.

She tugged his shirt off his shoulders and threw it on the floor. Then she was pressing herself against him, revelling in the way his skin felt against hers. Will's hand slid around her, cupping her breast and he kissed her, causing all kinds of turmoil inside her. Desire rose up in her like a flower opening.

As he was nearly a foot taller than her, she had to stand on her toes to meet his lips, but with each kiss, each caress, she swooned a little more, and the more blood rushed to the muscles between her legs, leaving less for her legs which were trying and failing to support her.

He slid his hands under her bottom and lifted her to him. Summer wrapped her legs around him, so they could hold one another tight, not breaking their bond. Groin to groin, he carried her to his room.

He laid her carefully on the bed, so carefully that Summer had to remind him, 'I'm fine, don't hold back.'

He regarded her from under heavy lids.

'I don't intend to,' she added.

His kisses scorched her skin, demolished her inhibitions. His lips teased down her dress, his hands explored under the hem and heaven help her when those same fingers found her underwear and began to stroke. Summer saw stars. And fireworks and any number of explosions.

She shifted away from under him, but only to shimmy out of her dress. Seeing this, Will kicked off his shoes and moved back to her.

Summer paused. His pants, his shorts. She'd dreamt of taking these off him. And now she was going to.

'I've wanted this for so long, you have no idea.' His voice was hoarse.

'I have some idea. I haven't exactly been keeping cool myself over here, you know?'

Summer unbuttoned his trousers and carefully eased them over his hips; she ran her palm over the front of his boxers, very much liking what she found there. He made a sound like a moan being stifled and her lips found his again. Kissing him was like magic. She loved the heavy look in his eyes, his lowered lids. He was unguarded, letting go. She was doing this to him.

How had she resisted so long? How had she ever thought this would be a mistake? It was glorious. She revelled in his touch, revelled in his reactions to her touch.

His lips traced a line of exquisite kisses from her earlobes to her nipples, sending her spiralling into an ever-increasing fever that would only be satisfied by one thing.

'Do you have protection?' she asked.

'Yes,' he mumbled, from his mouth's position between her breasts. 'But just a moment.'

How could he wait? She was ready to burst. Gorgeous, handsome Will, whose eyes made her muscles weaken and whose smile made them tighten again was laying kisses all over her body. She was helpless, hopeless, beneath him and at risk of falling completely apart. But with great effort, she held back. She wanted him, she wanted to join with him, to experience it with him. She could see the self-control etched across his face as they finally came together, loving her pleasure as much as his own.

Scrambling, scratching, climbing, chasing, until they reached the summit, one immediately behind the other. Looking into one another's eyes and understanding completely, they both let go.

What happens now?

Summer didn't voice the question aloud, but looked at Will the next morning, sprawled out on his bed next to her, messed up, crumpled. He'd never looked so gorgeous. He rolled over, smiled at her and her insides flipped again. God, he had an amazing smile. All the more precious because it still felt so rare. Will didn't smile easily, but when he did you knew he was sincerely happy.

As if he'd heard her unasked question, he said,

'So, you have a choice. You can leave on your flight tonight, as planned. But you could also stay.'

Stay? That wasn't part of any deal.

'The villa's booked for another night. But I don't have any meetings until the day after to-morrow. I could easily change our flights. See if we could get the villa for an extra night...' Will picked up her left hand and placed it between his. 'I'd like you to stay. With me.'

How often was she given the chance to spend two days in a tropical paradise with a gorgeous man? A gorgeous man she was beginning to have feelings for. Messy, complicated, impossible feel-ings. They may have shared an amazing night, but this moment was a crossroads. A point at which she should be sensible and go home as planned.

'We'd have two days. And then we'd go back to our own lives. Think of it as a stolen interlude before you start the rest of your life.'

Two days, no strings attached was the new deal he was offering. Which was good. It was all she could agree to. And she did want to stay. How could she possibly say no to forty-eight hours with Will?

Because every moment you stay, the more you're going to get used to this and the harder it is going to be to go back to the reality that is your life?

'It sounds lovely,' she heard her voice say.

'But?'

She shook her head. 'No buts. I'd love to stay.'

Love? Why did she use that word? 'Just let me check on some things at home.'

'Of course.' He placed a tender kiss on her shoulder. 'And while you're doing that, I'm not going to let that pool go to waste.'

She watched him get out of bed, still gloriously naked, and walk out the doors that led to the deck and the pool, not bothering with swimmers. And why would he, looking like he did? Strong, hard, and totally edible. This man made her body swoon and her heart sing.

Another night or two in Bali with him couldn't hurt, could it? They had lost time to make up for. They could have been sharing a bed all week, instead of worrying about their deal and some silly promise they'd made before they even knew one another. Now their work was over and they were free to enjoy themselves. And one another.

Summer reached for her phone. Penny didn't pick up the first time Summer called. She waited a few minutes and then tried again, urging her heart not to race. She knew she shouldn't panic at this point, there were all sorts of reasons why her mother wouldn't pick up right away, most of them benign. Penny picked up the second time and apologised.

'Sorry sweetheart. I couldn't get to my phone fast enough.'

'How are you, Mum?'

'Fine, fine.'

One 'fine' seemed to cancel out the other.

'Really, how are you feeling?'

'I'm doing great. But more importantly, how are you? Are you still flying home this evening?'

'That's what I was calling about. Um, another opportunity has come up.'

'Then you must take it.'

Her mother had no idea what sort of opportunity Summer was talking about, but Summer didn't enlighten her. 'It would just be for another two days and then I'd be home. Would you be okay with that?'

'Of course, that's okay, I can survive without you, you know?'

'I know.'

'You're a grown woman, you don't have to ask my permission. Stay. Make the most of it. I'd feel guilty if you missed an opportunity because of me.'

Summer knew that even if Penny understood the real reason she wanted to stay was to sleep in the arms of a handsome billionaire, her mother would still urge her to stay.

'Thanks, Mum, I'll send you my new flight details when I have them.'

'Have fun, sweetheart. You're only young once.'

Summer ended the call. Her mother was right. She was only young once. She glanced to the pool where Will was doing slow, lazy laps. His broad shoulders and long arms making short work of its length. The villa was completely private, high hedges shielded the pool where the villa did not. They were perched on a twenty-foot cliff, there was no chance of anyone looking in. Summer threw off the sheet and walked straight out to the deck and the edge of the pool.

Will turned when he reached the end of the pool, but when he noticed Summer, he almost swallowed a mouthful of water. She was standing at the other end of the pool, gloriously naked. Her beautiful hair surrounded her face like a halo. Lit up with the morning sun it looked as though she was on fire. Just like he was. His eyes travelled from hers down her gorgeous nose, to over her chin, which was tilted slightly up, as if in a challenge, down over the dip in her collarbone to her voluptuous breasts. His gaze skimmed her waist, which was the perfect size for his hands. He felt himself becoming hard again. Will couldn't remember ever being this turned on by a woman in his life and not just once, but over and over. There was no limit to his desire for her.

He stood, transfixed, blood pumping so hard through him, watching, savouring as she walked down the steps and entered the water.

'Everything okay?'

Please be okay, please stay.

She nodded. 'Everything's fine.'

She moved slowly through the water towards him. Even though it had been mere minutes since he'd touched her last, his body ached for her. Every second it took her to reach him was an exquisite torture.

And finally, the water parted and there she was. He reached for her, pulling her against him, cherishing the way the water caused a different friction against their skin, loving the way she was almost weightless as he lifted her up and she wrapped her legs around his waist, bringing their mouths level.

This was heaven. He could quite happily stay here for ever.

He couldn't stay there for ever though.

A while later, after they had tried the pool and then her bed, Will's phone pinged with a message from his mother asking if they would be joining everyone else for a late brunch.

'We should go, you know,' Summer said.

'I don't want to share you.'

She laughed. 'I want to go.'

'Haven't you had enough of my family? They aren't your responsibility any more.'

'Not at all. And it'll be different today.'

Not completely different, because they still weren't a couple. Not really. But he knew what she meant. It would be nice to see his family and not feel like a total fraud.

'It could be the last time I see Ben in a while too,' Will agreed.

* * *

They were the last to arrive at the brunch, but the first to leave. The mood was happy, but subdued, with most of the guests departing on an afternoon ferry and evening flights. The news that Will and Summer would be staying two extra nights was met with enthusiasm and envy.

When they finally hugged and kissed everyone goodbye, Will thought he saw Summer brush a tear from her cheek.

'What's up?'

'Nothing.' Summer shook her head and smiled. 'It's silly really. I won't see them again.'

'Ah.'

'And I know it wasn't real, I know that. But it's been fun. I've really liked getting to know them. You're very lucky, Will Watson.'

'I am,' he agreed, putting his arm around her, and pulling her closer. 'Don't think about that now. Let's enjoy this time.'

Maybe it was insensitive of him to dismiss her concern, but it was also the best thing to do. This was a brief moment they were carving out from the rest of their lives. Neither of them knew what would happen after and he didn't want to waste a minute of the next two days thinking about the future. For once he wanted to live in this exact moment. It was a new sensation for him. Not unpleasant, almost freeing.

For two days he'd forget his responsibilities—

he'd forget he was Will Watson, Businessman. For two days he would just be one half of Will and Summer.

And he liked that idea very much.

CHAPTER ELEVEN

THE LAST TWENTY-FOUR hours had been amazing. They had moved between the bed and the pool and the shower…and the bed again. And then the daybed by the pool. It had been both exhausting and exhilarating, Summer had never felt so satiated. Or alive. When it came to Will her desire seemed to have no limits.

But in less than twenty-four hours she'd be back at home. In the real world. The idea of seeing her mother, pulling on a pair of white satin flares, and climbing on stage seemed so strange and far away from this.

What if this was your life?

It wouldn't be; it couldn't be. Even Will had to return to the real world, or his rarefied version of it anyway. He still had a job, shareholders, a board to answer to. He had an important business to keep afloat, and not just for the sake of his bank balance, but for the sake of the rivers and the oceans. His work was about more than just making money, as she'd once believed.

Lying on her bed, Will dozed next to her. Summer slid her hand up his bare arm and her fingers reached the edge of his T-shirt. They crept up, under and to his strong biceps. Oh. Her fingertips felt their way over the tight ridges of his muscles. Will opened his eyes and reached for her, Summer straddled him and he rose to meet her lips. They kissed, fast, wild. Desire bloomed inside her and spread instantly through her torso. She ached for him and pressed herself closer to him. She tugged at his T-shirt, lifting it over his head.

He looked up at her, and the sparkle in his eyes nearly brought her undone.

'What's the rush?' he asked, but let her lift the shirt over his head.

'A week of sexual tension?' Summer lifted her own dress over her head and was glad she hadn't bothered to put on her bra again.

'A week?'

'What? You didn't feel it?'

'Summer.' Will's eyes went dark and serious. 'I've wanted you since I first saw you on that stage.'

The mood shifted from a frenzied rush to something more serious. His kisses became slower, more deliberate, as though each one was laced with meaning. This wasn't just fooling around, not for him and certainly not for her. Not any longer anyway.

They didn't take their eyes from one another,

she looked deep into his blue eyes as he moved inside her, feeling everything, noticing it all and committing all of it to memory. Wishing, foolishly, it could last for ever. Blocking out all the reasons why it couldn't and focusing on this moment alone, his touch, his smell, his breath on her neck, his fingers in her hair. Her body wanting to find its release, her heart wanting it to last for ever. Each stroke was more pleasurable than the last, each kiss more exquisite. His sighs reverberated inside her, her pleasure reflected in his eyes as they worked together, in unison to reach the climax.

After, they lay on her bed, her cheek resting on the magnificent work of art that was Will's chest and she absentmindedly played with the hair on his head.

'Would you like to see each other again? When we get home.' His voice wouldn't have drowned out a whisper.

Summer tried to open her mouth to respond, but her thoughts snagged. Was he suggesting a date? Or just a catch-up? Or something else? A relationship?

Given he was now naked and stroking her shoulder, she'd have to assume he meant the latter, but how could that be? Even if the contractual part of their relationship was over, he was still a billionaire and she was still a broke busker and unsuccessful songwriter.

Will pulled himself out from under her and his blue eyes met her green ones. 'You don't have to respond—you don't have to say anything now.'

She nodded. So he was talking about more than just a casual catch-up over coffee.

How would it work?

It was a little question, but with a huge answer.

And she had no idea where to begin.

Will loved the way Summer felt resting her head on his chest, her beautiful hair settled across his arms, his hand resting perfectly in the small of her back. His other hand held hers. The smell of the breeze, fresh off the ocean filled the room. The moment was perfect.

Except he'd gone and ruined it by asking her about the future. He'd asked on impulse, without thinking properly. The single thought he'd had at that moment had been, *I want to do this for ever.*

As soon as he'd asked if she'd like to see him again when they returned, he'd felt her body stiffen. And he'd remembered.

This was Summer. He cared about her too much for this to be just a fling, but did he really think that it could be anything else? The last time he'd fallen for someone he'd nearly lost everything. Summer wasn't Georgia, but there were still a million ways a relationship could go wrong.

This last week proved that; he'd told a lie and had come within a whisker of being found out.

Wasn't it best that he gave relationships a wide berth?

No one is talking about a relationship though, he reminded himself. He was just talking about dating. Seeing one another. Being with one another.

'If, just say, if, we do see one another back in Adelaide, how would it work?' she asked.

Will wasn't sure what she was getting at. 'We'd go on dates,' he said.

'I can't afford the places you go to. I can't afford to go out much at all.'

This was the least of their obstacles. He had money. He had too much money. 'And if I said that I'd pay?'

'I'd say that's very generous of you, and kind, but I can't be beholden to you.'

'You wouldn't be.' He wasn't expecting anything from her. There would be no contract, just him and her, together because they wanted to be.

'Yes, I would. You'd hold all the power.'

'I wouldn't be like that.'

'Saying it won't make it not true.'

'You told me you didn't care about money, only music. That's what you told me.'

She looked blank.

'In the letter you wrote me.' *The one I've kept with me every day since.*

'I was wrong. About so many things.' Summer pulled away from him and his body was bereft.

Will sat, tried to figure out what to say next,

but Summer grabbed a nearby robe and covered herself.

No!

He couldn't lose her. He'd pushed too fast, pressed too hard. He had to backtrack. He might not know what sort of future he wanted for them, but he knew one thing, he couldn't lose her. He'd had a glimpse of a world without Summer Bright in it two days ago and it had rocked him to his core.

They might not be able to have a serious relationship, but he wanted her in his life. In some wild, unpredictable way, he'd come to depend on her. Come to yearn for her. He liked the way he was when he was with her, he liked the way the world looked when he was with her. He might not know how to describe his feelings, but the one thing he was certain of was that he couldn't lose her.

'We don't need to decide anything now. We can just enjoy this time. I'm sorry I pressed. I know this is new. I just need you to know that I would like to see you again. I don't feel as though we're…finished.'

Summer pulled the robe tighter, but her gorgeous bottom landed back on the bed with a gentle thump.

She nodded and he breathed again.

'I don't feel as though we're finished either, but this does have an end date. We both know it.'

She clutched her hands together and twisted them in a way that made him want to grab them and soothe them and tell her everything would be okay.

But he wasn't sure if it would be.

Everything had an end date. Every contract, every deal, every relationship. He knew it as well as she did. The trick was always to find the right moment to exit. And he was no longer sure when that was. He had a feeling he was going to misjudge his next move and someone was going to get hurt.

'I shouldn't have brought it up. I'll only ruin what time we have left.' He needed to stop planning; he needed to be comfortable with not knowing his next move. Needing to predict and plan for the future had always been an essential skill to have in business. Not thinking about the future, even for a few moments was hard.

'The problem is, Will Watson, you've set such high expectations already.'

'What on earth do you mean?'

She threw her arms wide. 'I mean this! This place, this week. This afternoon. All of it. It's been wonderful.'

'And you don't think I can keep this kind of thing up?' he guessed.

'I'm sure neither of us can.'

'Could I at least try?'

He was serious, but she laughed.

'This is a holiday, for both of us. This isn't real. My life certainly doesn't consist of lying around an infinity pool in the tropical sun while I make love to a gorgeous and wonderful man.'

There was a message somewhere in her words but he only heard *gorgeous* and *wonderful*.

'And while I know your life has far more infinity pools and tropical sun than mine ever will, this isn't your real life either. Your real life is the office building I met you in. Where you look over the city and arrange business deals that effect everyone down below.'

Summer closed her eyes and paused, but he sensed she wasn't finished.

'I know that your role in the company isn't only important to everyone, it's important to you. And it's much more than just a job, it's your life.'

Was his life so incompatible with hers? She wouldn't be by his side at the charity events he attended, she'd be on the stage. Her financial position didn't bother him, but the difference between them clearly bothered her. For the first time he really saw it wasn't nothing. He imagined their situations reversed and felt cold. She was right. Here, in Bali, away from the real world, they could make things work. But back in Adelaide they wouldn't make sense.

He took a deep breath. He didn't like the conclusion he'd just reached, but that was too bad.

Live in the moment.

'So, we have one night left in Bali. Money is no object—I'm sorry to remind you, but it isn't— what would you like to do?'

'Now you're talking.'

'We could get someone in to make us an amazing dinner. Or we could go out to one of the restaurants. We could even get a boat over to the main island and explore some more.'

Summer pressed her lips together thoughtfully. If it was up to him, they'd spend every second they had left together in this villa, but he knew that Summer might never come back to Bali again. He also knew that if they did spend the next twenty-four hours wrapped in each other's bodies it was going to be even more difficult to untangle themselves when they arrived back home.

'Yes, that. I'd love to see some more.'

'Great,' he said, hoping he sounded sincere. 'I'll make a call or two.'

Will climbed out of bed, looking for his phone. He was still naked and noticed Summer watching him, colour high in her cheeks and a cheeky smile on her face. He wanted to burst. He also wanted to fall back onto the bed and pull her to him.

'We should get dressed,' he said before he was too tempted to do just that.

'Into what?'

'Something suitable for an amazing evening.'

Will made some calls and was assured that everything would be taken care of. He showered and dressed and tapped his fingers on his knee while he waited for her.

Live in the moment. Live in the moment.

Summer came out of her room and he was powerless to stop his jaw dropping.

'I got this in Ubud,' she said, doing a twirl. She wore a floor-length halter-neck dress, loose and flowing, just like her fiery hair around her shoulders.

She was amazing.

They shouldn't work, but they did.

No, he reminded himself. This wasn't real life.

Summer had no idea what Will had planned for them and he was keeping the plans close to his chest. And what a chest it was, covered now in a loose blue linen shirt, with the sleeves rolled up. She picked up his hand to stop herself from sliding her hand over his chest and through the opening where his top two buttons were undone to feel the firmness behind it. The man was edible and for a moment she regretted her decision for them to go out exploring the island. They should be back in the villa exploring one another's bodies.

They were picked up at the villa by a taxi and driven to the small port on the island.

'Where are we going?'

'It's a surprise,' he said.

But as soon as they were shown onto a private speedboat, their pilot asked, 'You're going to Nusa Dua?'

Will nodded.

Summer knew Nusa Dua was one of the most exclusive enclaves on the main island with luxury hotels and restaurants. Gus and Diane had contemplated having their wedding there but chose instead the more relaxed and casual atmosphere of Nusa Lembongan.

'I thought we could have an explore and then I've booked us dinner.'

'Wonderful.'

And it was.

The boat sped them across the bay and delivered them to Nusa Dua, its beautiful beaches, lined with palm trees and never-ending greenery. A car took them to a clifftop temple, where they got out to look more closely at the beautiful shrine. They were then delivered to a luxury restaurant overlooking the Indian Ocean and another magnificent Bali sunset. Pinks and oranges faded to purples and dark blues and finally the stars appeared. The open-air restaurant was lit with lanterns and candles.

Will couldn't have picked a more perfect destination if he'd tried. After a dinner that was probably one of the most delicious Summer had eaten in her life of lobster and barramundi and everything else besides, they watched a live show of

Balinese dancers accompanied by a gamelan, an ensemble of Balinese instruments.

Though all of that was just window dressing. The most special part of the evening was simply being with Will. She kept wondering how easy it would be to let herself be swept along with the tide that was Will Watson. To let him take care of everything…

No, she reminded herself. *Because when you surrender yourself like that you risk everything.* And she wasn't going to end up like her mother. Or put herself in the position she'd let herself get into with Michael. She wouldn't let herself depend so much on another. Being with Will would mean doing that. He was so larger than life, his presence, his fortune so much, she felt in danger of forgetting who she was.

She wouldn't. Because by the time the sun set tomorrow, she would have said goodbye to Will for ever.

As the sun rose over their last morning in Bali and the room was gradually filled with a soft pink light, Will was still wide awake.

He hadn't slept a second. Hadn't lost consciousness for a moment. Every time he'd felt his mind drifting off, he'd been jolted awake again and felt Summer in his arms. Looked at her. Breathed in her scent.

He didn't want to miss a moment of it. Of

her. Summer now lay curled around him and he watched her back rise and fall with each breath she took, his own in time with hers. Breathing in the same air, being in the same beautiful bubble.

If this was all the time they had, he was going to be there for every second. When the sun was higher in the sky and the light had brightened, Summer began to stir. Her glorious body moved against his and she lifted herself to look at him. She gave him an unfocused, drowsy smile and his heart twisted.

'Good morning, sweet pea,' he said.

'Good morning, honey.'

'Is it time?' she asked.

Not, what is the time? But is it time? Is it all over?

'Nearly. Breakfast will be here soon and we get picked up in about two hours.'

Summer rolled over and Will resisted the urge to pull her back. It was better this way.

'I'll just have a shower.'

'Good idea,' he said but his voice cracked.

It was a truly terrible idea. The only good idea was for her to lie back down with him and stay for ever. But that wasn't to be. She climbed out of bed and went to the bathroom, closing the door behind herself.

The breakfast was delivered while he was in the shower and he came out to find Summer dressed and finishing off hers.

She stood when he entered. 'I've had my break-fast. I'll go and finish packing.'

His heart fell. It was as though it was already over.

It is over, he reminded himself.

He shouldn't have let it go on this far because saying goodbye to Summer was going to be harder than he'd imagined. But he'd have to. He didn't know how to convince her that they should see one another back home. Summer saw his fortune as a barrier. Not only his money, but his entire life. She wasn't expecting him to give anything up—and nor was he—but even he had to admit he didn't know how to make their lives fit together. He'd spent years negotiating all kinds of deals, solving all kinds of problems, but the one time he really needed to be persuasive all his powers failed him.

On the ferry across to the main island, they were both slightly subdued, which was to be ex-pected due to their lack of sleep. Despite spend-ing the majority of the past thirty-six hours in bed neither of them was well rested. Their con-versation was stilted, about practical matters only. Will's emotions were churning inside him and he felt queasy.

It's just the ferry ride, he reasoned, even though he'd never had any kind of seasickness before in his life.

CHAPTER TWELVE

THE FLIGHT BACK was far more subdued than the trip over. They didn't quiz one another; they hardly talked. And Summer certainly wasn't filled with anticipation about what would happen when they landed.

Fed up with the silence, somewhere over the centre of Australia she turned to Will and said, 'Someone once told me that a debrief is an essential part of any project.'

'A post-mortem?'

'It didn't go that badly, did it?' She smiled, but didn't feel it. 'What does one talk about during a debrief?'

'Usually we would talk about what went well, what we learnt.'

'I think we convinced your family that we're a couple, so that went well.'

'A little too well,' he mumbled.

She knew what he meant. Diane, Gus, Ben and Charlotte had all liked her and embraced her into their family. She'd become close to them. Her chest ached at the thought she'd never see any of them again.

'What did you learn?' she asked. She wasn't ready to tell him that the main lesson she'd take away from this week was never get involved in a fake relationship with a gorgeous billionaire. Not that it was a life lesson that was going to be particularly useful in the future.

'Ah.' He rubbed his chin, still covered in a light stubble. She liked it on him. It made him look softer, more relaxed. More approachable. Clean-shaven, Will was undoubtedly heart-stoppingly handsome, but with messy hair, a few days growth he was…hers.

She shook her head. He'd never be hers.

'I learnt that I can still be surprised by people.'

She couldn't help but smile. 'I did too.'

Will had surprised her, every day. She was right about many things, but so wrong about others as well. His tenderness, his ability to make her laugh. The way he seemed to genuinely care about her.

The way that despite their many differences, they still had so much to talk about.

The way he could do things to her in the bedroom that no one had ever been able to do. She'd thought that artists and musicians were her thing, but it turned out that business tycoons were also her kink.

'Anything else in a debrief?' Maybe he could

tell her how to move on from this. How to say goodbye without it hurting so much.

'What we'd do better next time.'

'Next time?'

He reddened. They were back to this conversation. She wanted to see him again, but knew it was pointless. It would only hurt more to say goodbye to him in another week or two or however long it took to become glaringly apparent to him they would not work as a couple back in the real world.

'My mother's asked us around for dinner when they get back from their honeymoon. In about a month.'

'Oh.' What was he saying? He wasn't suggesting a date, or a catch-up. But to see his family.

They'd talked about this, hadn't they? No, they'd agreed to talk about it later, though Summer had said all she could say. She might want to see him again, but it was best for both of them in the long run if they didn't.

'That wasn't part of the deal,' she said.

'You set fire to that, remember?'

'The other deal we agreed to was forty-eight hours only. And you're threatening to break that one.'

'I'm a ruthless businessman, what can I say?' He held up his hands in surrender and grinned. She smiled too, even though her heart was breaking. How could that be?

'I don't think that dragging it on any longer

than we have already is going to help either of us in the long run. We're too different.'

'Not really.'

'Our lives are too different. You run a billion-dollar business. I busk on the street. I have responsibilities.'

'Your mother.'

'Yes, and that's not nothing.'

'I didn't say it was. I just mean that we can overcome all those things.'

Will cupped her chin in his hands. She wanted to believe him. She wanted to rest her head on his shoulder, for everything to be okay, for everything to make sense.

'I don't belong in your world,' she said.

'How can you say that? I've been beside you all week, remember, watching you in my world as you call it. I've seen you with my mother, my family. Everyone. They adore you. You do belong in my life. As much as I do anyway.'

'What does that mean?'

'It means…' Will dragged his hand across his head. 'I don't always feel that I belong either. But with you, I do.'

'Because this is your world, Will, not mine. Mine is worrying about how I'm going to meet the rent, looking after my mother, hoping my next gig doesn't get cancelled.'

'If you were with me…'

'You can't support me, Will—that's what I'm

trying to say. You can't support me and my mother. And if we were dating and you were paying for everything that's what it would feel like. It's okay for you to pay in Bali, but not back at home. It wouldn't feel right to me.'

'I...'

'Will, it's like I asked yesterday, how would it work? Going on a date every now and then? Or not going on dates, just hiding out in your apartment? Keeping our lives separate?'

'Yes, if that's what you want.'

But it wasn't what she wanted. She didn't want to simply see one another on the rare times their schedules allowed. She didn't want a fight every time about where they went and what they did and who paid. And she certainly didn't want to have a secret relationship, one where they never went out.

She wanted someone who was looking to the future with her. They didn't have to know everything, they didn't have to make lifelong promises, but they needed to be looking in the same direction. Most importantly of all, they needed to be able to share their lives together. Summer wanted a life partner. And she needed more than just an offer to go on a few dates.

She shook her head. 'I don't want a part-time boyfriend, Will.'

'That's not what I'm saying. I'm saying you can trust me.'

She was woken from the dream, confused, blinded by the clarity of what he'd just said. She'd be the one having to trust him, she had so much to lose, more than him.

Trust. It was a funny thing. 'Trust you? Will, we've been lying all along.'

'But not to one another. Of course you can trust me, I'm not going to steal from you, now am I?'

Summer's heart fell. Then rose again, but filled with hurt. And a bit of rage. She sat firmly back in her own seat.

'Meaning, what? I might steal from you?'

'I didn't say that and that's not what I meant. I trust you, Summer.'

She wanted to believe him, but to do so would be repeating the mistakes of the past. This was still the same Will Watson who was so terrified of trusting another person that he'd invented a fake girlfriend so his mother would stop setting him up with eligible women.

The same Will Watson who had been lying to his family and his shareholders ever since. The same Will Watson who had made her sign a four-page contract just for one week away together.

He would never trust a penniless singer like her.

'This is exactly what I meant last night. We're not equals.'

'Of course we're equals.'

'You own half of Adelaide. As of tomorrow, I'll have one old guitar to my name.'

'Summer, I trust you.'

She closed her eyes. She wanted to believe him. And she was convinced that he believed himself. But they both had to face the truth, it wouldn't work. Will was right, if it was simply the difference in their financial positions to overcome there might be a way through.

But it was more than that.

She would not let herself fall for him. She would not let herself rely on him. As soon as she fell for him, he'd have the power to break her.

It's too late though, isn't it?

She sat like that for a while, her eyes closed, unable to look at him. The significance of this realisation almost crushing her with its weight.

She loved him. He made her laugh, she loved his drive, she loved his smile. She loved his quirks. She absolutely adored him.

'Summer,' he said after a while. 'I don't know what to say. I don't know how to make this better.'

She picked up his hand. 'I know, Will, it's okay. I think we both need to accept this is our fate and move on. It'll be easiest in the long run.'

She couldn't love him. She wouldn't. Loving Will, giving herself to him would probably destroy her once and for all.

'Summer! Sweetheart!' Penny exclaimed when Summer pushed open the door and dragged in her bag. A suitcase which a week ago felt light and now weighted a ton. Just like her heart.

She looked around the unit; washing was piled in the sink and the place needed a tidy. She didn't blame her mother; she knew Penny had good days and bad days. Summer felt guilty for leaving her mother over what she now realised had been one of the bad weeks.

'You haven't been telling me the truth, have you, Mum?'

'I don't know what you mean,' Penny replied.

'Every day when I called, you said you were doing fine.'

'And I have been fine. I've been managing.'

Summer sighed. They had different definitions of *managing*.

'Well, I'm not going to go away again anytime soon.'

'It didn't go well? You said your performance was a success.'

'Oh, yes, it was.'

From the point of view of the deal it had been a raging success. From the point of view of her heart, it had been an abject failure. Summer started picking up glasses and mugs from the living room and carried them to the kitchen, where she started washing up.

'At least unpack first!' Penny called out, but Summer wanted to keep her hands busy and found the routine of cleaning soothing. She tidied the apartment, started a load of washing and then looked in the fridge to figure out what they would eat for dinner.

'Come and sit for a moment.' Penny pointed to the couch next to her.

Summer brought her mother a cup of tea and sat.

'I could say the same to you about not telling the truth.'

'What do you mean?'

Her mother gave her a knowing look.

'But I have,' she said.

Her mother eased an eyebrow and Summer's spine slumped.

'Okay, no. I may have left out a few details.'

It all came out. Meeting Will, the deal, meeting his family. How they'd grown closer. How he wasn't the uptight money-obsessed man she'd initially thought him to be. She told her about being swamped by the wave, leaving out some of the details. She told her about the wedding and how she and Will had decided to stay two extra days, leaving a few of those details out too.

Then she'd told her mother how when Will had asked to see her again, back in Adelaide, she'd said no.

'But why? You clearly care about him.'

Yes, she did. And that was the whole point. 'It could never work.'

'Why not?'

'Why not? Because he's a super successful businessman, Mum.'

'So? How is that a bad thing?'

'Because I'm me!'

'And what's wrong with you? Nothing.'

Spoken like a true mother.

'It's not that I don't feel worthy of him. I don't
want to be dependent on him.'

'Why would you have to be? You're not talking about moving in together already, are you?'

Summer shook her head.

'I feel that he's so…successful, so much more
than I am. His life is together and mine just isn't.
I feel as though I might be in danger of being
swept away and lost. Somehow.'

'Are you talking about money, or something
else?'

'Money is important.'

'Heavens, I'm not saying it isn't. But are you
using his money as an excuse?'

'No. But it isn't nothing.' Will had also suggested that his fortune wasn't a relevant consid-
eration in any of this. But it was a huge barrier
between them. An immovable elephant blocking
the road forward.

'All of it. He's been hurt before, betrayed. He's
got even less reason to trust me. And how can I
trust him? How can I possibly believe that he won't
get sick of me one day?'

Penny pulled a face. 'When did you get to be so cynical?'

'I'm not cynical. I'm realistic, Mum. You know as well as I do that relationships end. One person always ends up hurting the other. One person always ends up misjudging the other.'

Penny shook her head. 'I know I haven't been the best example, made the best choices. But I never said no to love. I never stopped believing in it. Not even now. Especially not now.'

Summer looked at her mother. She was bed-ridden some days; she found it hard to leave the flat. She still believed in love.

'He'll get sick of me one day.'

'Oh, Summer, I can't believe I'm hearing you speak this way. Do you honestly think that just because he's rich, that he thinks differently to you? That he sees you differently?'

'I *know* he thinks differently. I know his priorities are different to mine.'

'I've never heard you so down on yourself.'

'I'm not down on myself. That's *not* what it's about. It's just about the fact that we live in different worlds.'

'As far as I can see, you both live in this one. Not to mention the same city.'

'Mum, we met because I sang at a charity dinner he was at. He paid thousands of dollars to attend. I was paid four hundred. How is it supposed to work?'

'I thought you were more imaginative than this.'

'What's imagination got to do with it? How's that going to help with dealing with reality?' Summer's skin felt hot and she was suddenly aware that she'd worked her heart rate up to dangerous levels. She needed a break, she needed to take a moment to calm herself.

Penny looked at her with concern. 'You've had a long trip; you should have a rest.'

Summer nodded. She did need a rest. She needed to fall asleep and forget about Will for a few hours. And then tomorrow she needed to start forgetting him all over again.

The next day Summer woke before the sun rose, but rather than lie in bed and wait for sleep she knew wouldn't come, she got up and got to work. The first thing she needed to do was buy back her guitar and rig.

She arranged a time to meet Brayden then she got the bus to a cafe near his house. Brayden had the decency to look embarrassed by the situation, but she knew it wasn't his fault. It was Michael's. And he had been decent enough to hold on to the guitar while Summer gathered the money together.

'What's the best price you can offer me?' Summer asked, emboldened by the fact the guitar was sitting right there.

'I thought we agreed on seven-seven.'

'But what's the best you can do? You can't have paid Michael seven-seven.'

Brayden looked sheepish. Summer held her ground even as her insides were turning to mush. He could just pick up the things and leave.

But he didn't. 'Six thousand. I paid six thousand. I didn't know they were stolen.'

'How about I give you six-five. For your time. You still come out ahead.'

Brayden nodded and finally, finally, she held her guitar again.

And she hadn't rolled over. She'd argued for a better deal. She'd stood her ground and she felt like she could fly.

She now had enough change left over from Will's money to take her mother shopping for a new outfit and maybe some books she'd been wanting to read. Will's money was not going to be spent on bills; it was going to be spent on things that would make them happy.

Summer carried her guitar on her back and wheeled her rig home. One of the reasons for the high price tag of the rig was its light weight and portability. Even as she made her way back across town with it, it felt weightless. And she felt surprisingly light. The song she had started in Bali was coming to her now, also effortlessly, naturally.

It was unfortunate, she thought, that her best songs inevitably came to her when she was heartbroken.

There would be other heartbreaks and there would be joy again in her life, but after this song. She needed to get this song out of her and onto paper, into the air and out into the world. Once this one was finished and sung and out there then she could say goodbye to its subject once and for all.

It was a love letter to Will and a paean to heartbreak. It was about wanting something you knew you could never have.

CHAPTER THIRTEEN

'SUMMER WON'T BE COMING,' Will said.

Diane had returned from her honeymoon a few weeks ago and Will had been avoiding her, but she'd tracked him down in the one place he couldn't really avoid her: his office.

'Why not?' Diane asked.

Will had been dreading this moment since the airport. He'd been dreading a lot of things since he'd watched Summer wheel her small bag away from him at the Adelaide Airport without turning back. He dreaded facing each day without her; he dreaded going home from the office to his empty apartment. He dreaded spending the evenings alone. And most of all he found himself dreading waking up each morning and feeling the cold of the bed next to him.

But he'd also been dreading this moment and telling his mother the truth.

He knew he didn't have to tell her everything, but he also knew that if he didn't at least tell her, he'd still be lying in one way and he was tired.

He was sick of pretending that everything was okay when it wasn't.

'We broke up,' he said. And it wasn't really a lie.

'Oh, darling.' Diane went to him and wrapped her arms around him. 'What happened? You both seemed so happy.'

'That's just the thing. We weren't.'

'Don't be silly. I saw the way you looked at one another.'

'Mum, there's something I have to tell you and I'm not proud of it. I would like to tell you the truth and I know that you'll be upset. I am very sorry for it and I know you'll be disappointed, but please know I did it for you.'

Diane crossed her arms and narrowed her eyes.

'I made Summer up.'

Diane laughed. 'What do you mean you made her up?'

'When I told you I had a girlfriend and that her name was Summer, I made that up.'

'Summer isn't her name?'

'No, Summer is her name, but I invented a girl-friend called Summer Bright believing that no one in Adelaide would have such a name. But I should've checked because one does and we ran into her that night at the charity dinner.'

'I don't believe you,' Diane said. 'She is real. I found her. I booked her band for the gala.'

'I'm telling you the truth.'

Diane shook her head. 'No, that's too much of a coincidence, you must've met her before.'

'I hadn't met her. Our paths had never crossed.'

'Okay, so you made her up, but then you met, and she came to Bali. She came to my wedding.'

'Because I asked her to.' Will stopped, took a few deep breaths, but still sought to find the courage he needed to tell his mother the next part. 'We made a deal. She'd come to Bali and pretend to be my girlfriend for a week and I agreed to pay her almost eight thousand dollars.'

He couldn't read the look on his mother's face that moment. Incredulity? Amusement? Disgust? Maybe all three.

'I still don't believe you,' she said.

Will begin to pace. Why wouldn't she believe him?

'I'm honestly telling you the truth. I didn't have to, but I feel like I owe it to you to tell you.'

'So, you're saying you were pretending the whole time? I saw you hold hands. I saw you laugh together. I saw the way you looked at her. I saw how terrified you were when you returned from the medical centre. I've never seen you that shaken. Not even when your father died.'

'I felt responsible for that, it was my fault.'

Diane shook her head. 'Are you really saying it was all made up?'

'We did become close. We became friends.'

'Oh, there you go.' Diane put her palms on her knees and went to stand, as if that settled it.

'I wanted to see her again, I hoped we would, but we're just too different.'

'Nonsense. Everyone's different. Differences are what make couples work. Look at Gus and I.'

'It's not just that.'

Will looked down but felt his mother's gaze on him. 'I'm sorry for lying.'

Diane made a noise he couldn't interpret. 'Darling, I'm not entirely convinced that you did.'

Will said goodbye to his mother and tried to put the conversation out of his mind. He'd confessed, come clean and if she didn't believe him, well what was he supposed to do? Just get on with his life and try and forget the whole sorry business.

Two days later Will was turning his desk upside down to search for his phone charger. It wasn't plugged into the outlet where it usually was and he couldn't remember if he'd moved it or not.

Ever since Bali he'd been more disorganised than usual. Losing things. Almost forgetting appointments. It was just the break that had done it; his routine was out and it would come back soon.

As would his sleep.

And his appetite.

Since Bali he'd woken at 2:00 a.m. every morning, discombobulated, sweaty, almost panicky. Like he'd forgotten something important. He'd toss and turn for hours, only drifting off to sleep shortly before his alarm. The sleep deprivation was the likely cause of his forgetfulness during the day. And probably the loss of appetite as well. He didn't even feel like swimming any more, even though the days were hotter and the water was getting warmer.

He didn't feel like doing much at all.

Since Bali.

Since Summer.

It was silly; he and Summer didn't belong together so he shouldn't be so tied up about her. Logically they didn't have anything in common. On paper they didn't add up. He shouldn't feel like this. He should be able to sleep; he shouldn't feel like everything he ate tasted of cardboard.

He had enough self-awareness to realise that he wasn't doing great, but what else could he do? He couldn't call Summer; he certainly couldn't ask to see her. If he did, he'd be right back where he was a month ago. Not sleeping at all and yet still not wanting to get out of bed. He had to just let time work its special healing magic and keep putting one foot in front of the other until it did.

Starting with finding the damn phone charger.

He opened the bottom drawer of his desk, not really believing it would be in there. This drawer was simply full of bits and pieces he didn't really need but had never been bothered to throw out.

It wouldn't be in this drawer because he was

sure he hadn't even opened this drawer since his desk was carried in here from his old office.

And sure enough, it wasn't. There was a phone charger, but belonging to a phone he hadn't owned in five years. There was a program from a conference he'd been to years ago and for some reason decided to keep, probably because it had sparked an idea that he hadn't pursued.

He pushed the program aside and froze. Beneath it was a business card. He reached for it, not sure what he was seeing, not sure if he was hallucinating, but then slowly, as if remembering a dream later in the day, he knew.

It was a simple business card, with a guitar, an email address, and a name. Summer Bright.

How did that get here? Even as he asked himself the question, he knew the answer. He'd picked it up, that's how. He'd seen a busker in the Bourke Street Mall one day and stopped. Partly because he'd been in a contemplative mood, partly because he'd really liked her sound, her singing. And her looks.

He'd tossed her twenty dollars and picked up one of her cards, intending to look her up and see if he could download her songs.

He'd chuckled when he'd seen her name, Summer Bright.

It suited her. And her songs, which were joyful and upbeat, but still clever and moving.

Yes, he'd vowed he'd try and find her songs because standing out there, in the sunshine, listening to her he'd felt happier and more fulfilled than he had in ages.

He'd practically skipped back upstairs, only to walk back into some crisis or another that had needed his immediate attention. The card had ended up in his bottom drawer and he hadn't thought of her again.

Except he had.

When his mother had asked the name of his fake girlfriend he'd said her name was Summer Bright.

And not because of the weather or the sun or anything else, but because her name was still lurking in his subconscious, waiting patiently for him to remember that she was there.

That she existed.

No matter how many times Summer looked down into her guitar case, she still couldn't believe it. It was filled with money. And not just loose silver change but notes. Of all colours. Not to mention all the people who had tapped on her QR code to give payments of five dollars. The code sat on the new stand, next to her business cards and next to a photo of Nina Sparrow, who last week had contacted her asking if Summer would help write her new album.

Nina Sparrow was probably the biggest pop star in the country right now. She'd recently broken through into the American market, increasing her fame to stratospheric levels.

A few weeks ago, Summer had uploaded one of her new songs to social media. The one she had written about Will. The exercise had really been one to prove to herself that she had her guitar back, but the song had managed to catch people's attention and once it caught on it was like a runaway truck. So many people had listened to it. Including Nina Sparrow.

Nina's unique blend of folk and pop was a perfect fit for Summer's style. She'd asked if she could record the song, and whether Summer would help her write a few more for her upcoming release.

Summer had given her a cautious yes.

After so many years of setbacks, disappointments and near misses, this was, she knew, it. She wouldn't make the same mistakes she'd made last time; she'd already engaged a lawyer to look over the contract Nina was offering.

She'd thought about contacting Will. The deal with Nina was noteworthy enough that she considered letting him know so she could thank him and let him know that if it were not for the money she'd made she wouldn't have done it.

But she'd never hit Send on the message. Because it wasn't just the guitar that he'd contributed to her new success, it was the song itself.

The song she'd written about him.

Thanks for breaking my heart. I wrote a great song because of it.

No.

If he heard the song, maybe he'd think of her. Maybe he'd never even know that she wrote it and that was for the best. She didn't really want him knowing. She didn't want him to think that he had anything to feel sorry for.

The crowd before her wasn't moving. It was after five and people should be heading home. Or to the beach, to make the most of the warmer weather. But a patient and persistent group of people were waiting for her to sing The Song. The one she almost hadn't uploaded. The one that, against all expectations and odds had gone viral. The song that would signal the turning point in Summer's life.

The problem was she didn't yet trust herself to sing it without tearing up. It had been hard enough to sing it for the recording she'd posted. Yesterday, on this same spot, she'd pretty much fallen to pieces. But she had to try.

Besides, this was the song that would launch her career; she'd have to listen to Nina singing it and then hopefully, hear it being played on radio stations around the world. She had to make herself immune to the emotions and memories it evoked.

It was getting late and she needed to get home

to her mother. It was now or never. She could sing it. She had to. She also had to live the rest of her live without Will—what was one silly song?

She drew a deep breath and said, 'I think this is the one you've all been waiting for.' And she strummed the opening.

You can do this. You can do this.

It was the mantra she told herself every morning when her alarm went off, always way too early.

You made the right decision.

Then she sang the opening words. *'It just wasn't meant to be...'*

Saying goodbye to Will had hurt more than the woman who had first sung to him dressed up as one quarter of ABBA could have ever imagined. More than the woman who had signed the contract across his back could ever have believed.

'It wasn't you...it wasn't me...'

Will had broken her heart, but he'd also given her so much. He'd inspired her hit song, but he'd given her the confidence and the nous to make sure that this time she wasn't cheated out of her rightful dues.

'I had to let you go...'

Summer reached the bridge and the key change and she saw him. Her voice cracked on the next note and she had to turn away. When she reached the end of the next chorus she looked back in his direction, hoping he'd be gone. Or maybe he hadn't been there at all. Just a figment of her emotions.

But he was still there and held her gaze with his.

He'd heard her song and no doubt knew it was about him. The lyrics *'We faked it until we made it'* alone would've given it away. She contemplated going over to him and telling him it was about another fake relationship she'd had recently, but that would be too ridiculous, even for her.

'Thank you all very much for listening, have a great night,' she said as soon as she'd strummed the final note.

There was applause and also a few calls for 'encore' but she shook her head and placed her guitar in its case. The crowd gradually dispersed, many of them tapping on her QR code as they went. She busied herself packing up, not daring to look in his direction, but conscious he was still standing there.

'Nice rig,' he said. 'The guitar sounds great.'

She forced herself to look at him and smile. She had to be brave. 'Thanks very much to you.'

'The song is great.'

'Thanks.'

Oh, no. He knew the song was about him and he was going to say something. Her heart wasn't just broken, it was ripped from her chest and smeared all over the song for all the world to see.

'No one knows the song is…that is.' She lowered her voice, 'It isn't *just* about you.'

Will's face reddened, but he stayed standing

there, looking at her, shifting his weight from foot to foot.

She thought the worst thing had been walking away from him, but in terms of embarrassment and mortification, *this* was by far the worst. Standing before him right now, knowing that he knew how much he'd hurt her. And that the world knew too. He was wearing the full catastrophe, suit, business shirt and jacket, even in the heat. His outfit helped. A little. It put a bit of distance between them, this was business Will. Not shorts and T-shirt Will. Not naked by the pool Will.

That was the Will she missed most of all.

What was the etiquette in this situation? Hands-down there was not a greeting card that had a pre-prepared message for this moment. 'I'm sorry the song I wrote about our brief affair is now viral on social media. And I'm sorry it's going to be played everywhere in the world once Nina Sparrow, one of the biggest artists in the world, records her version.'

She had to leave, get home. Most of all, she had to leave Will behind, once and for all. But he wasn't moving. He was waiting for something.

'What are you doing here?' she asked.

He held up her business card. One of the ones that now sat on the stand next to her Square.

Summer Bright
Singer, songwriter, performer

There was an image of a guitar and her social media handle.

'You came to get one of my cards? You have my details.'

'No, I didn't just pick it up. I came to show it to you.'

'I don't understand. Where did you get it?'

'I found it in my desk drawer.'

'I didn't put it there.'

He smiled. 'No, you didn't. I did. Two years ago, when I first saw you busking on this corner. I've walked past you many times.'

'I still don't understand,' she said.

'I didn't make you up, Summer Bright. I *remembered* you. You were in my subconscious. Waiting there all along. When my mother asked who I was seeing, I didn't pull the name from nowhere, I was remembering you.'

'On purpose?' She still didn't understand what he was saying. Or even why he was here.

'No, because I was too silly. I saw you busking. I liked you. I picked up your card, so I could remember you, look up your songs. But I put it away and forgot about it. Except I didn't really.'

Summer let this all sink in. It was sweet. And bizarre. But it didn't change anything between them.

He worked in the sky; she worked on the ground.

'I know you have a lot to lose, but I do too. You have my heart, Summer Bright. I don't give that away easily, but you have mine and you'll have it for ever. Please be kind to it.'

'What about my heart?' Summer didn't know where those words had come from or how she'd let down her guard enough to say them.

'I will hold your heart, cherish it, protect it and love it, for ever.'

Relief, joy, rushed through her. Could it work? Could *they* work?

We'll fake it until we make it...

He'd collected her card years ago and held on to it. Because he'd wanted to know more about her. He hadn't chosen her name because he thought it was ridiculous, he'd plucked it from his subconscious because he'd remembered her. Remembered enough about her to wonder if she would be a good girlfriend for him.

He was right.

She was good for him.

She looked at him now more closely. Past the suit. His face was drawn, with dark circles growing under his eyes. He wasn't wearing a tie. His hair wasn't combed. He looked real.

And she wanted him. She'd always wanted him since she'd noticed him in the crowd that night from the stage.

He was beautiful. And he was hers.

She rushed to him, threw her arms around him and he caught her. Strong and sure. Her Will.

He pulled her tight and she pressed her face

into his chest, breathing him in with deep breaths to catch her own breath but also to prove to herself that he was here, with her. Holding her. Loving her. She never wanted to let him go.

Will eased her face away and looked her in the eyes. 'I love you, Summer. I don't want to be apart from you again. I know there are things we need to figure out, I know—'

'I love you too.'

Will's expression broke into the most beautiful smile she'd ever seen, gooey and warm. And so Will.

He leant down again and pressed his lips tenderly to hers, sealing their declarations. But as soon as they both understood, she pulled him tighter, her insides curling with need and a months' worth of pent-up longing. Will pulled her tight and fell easily into the kiss. She was vaguely aware that they were standing on a busy street corner in peak hour but she didn't care. The only important thing in the world right now was Will.

A wolf whistle intruded into their bubble and they pulled back, panting.

Will said, 'I know there are things to work through, but I also know we can work things out.'

'Of course, you're an expert planner. But please, no spreadsheets this time.'

His brow furrowed, 'Really?' then his expression broke into a grin. 'If you insist.'

'I was scared,' she confessed.

'I was too. You need to know that I might be successful but I can still be stupid sometimes.'

'You weren't stupid. I just didn't see how someone like you could be with someone like me.'

Serious, Will held her back at a distance and said, 'I think you're perfect the way you are.'

'I think you're perfect too.'

The peak hour crowd swirled around them.

'I think it might be time to go somewhere a little more private.'

'I'd like that.'

Will helped her pack away her guitar and rig, but when his eyes landed on the photo of Nina Sparrow he asked, 'Why have you got this here?'

Summer told him about the song and the offer. 'And I've got someone to look over it this time.'

Will beamed. 'I'm so happy for you. Not for getting someone to check the contract, but for the deal. It's so fantastic. I'm sorry I didn't know before this.' He looked down. 'Honestly, I've had to stop myself from checking what you've been up to.'

She picked up his hand. 'I understand. I've been doing the same thing. But you should know, the song, I wrote it about you.'

'So, the world knows what a fool I am?'

Summer laughed. 'No, they know that we were both afraid, but...'

'Yes?'

'In the next song they'll know that we're madly in love.'

'And that we will figure out how to make our lives fit together.'

'And that we're learning how to be brave.'

He kissed her again.

EPILOGUE

'IT'S SO BIG,' Summer said as she threw her arms wide and looked around again at the magnificent room, all the more special for the view of the ocean it offered. 'Do we really need this much space?'

'I think we do.'

Summer had been spending most of her time at Will's spacious penthouse apartment, which was several orders of magnitude larger than her flat, but he was insisting they needed their own place.

It was true, she did still think of Will's apartment as his, even though she spent more nights there than not. It was nice that he wanted a place that was theirs.

Still. This place was massive.

'I think we do this,' he said. 'It's a good price, and a great spot.'

The beach was barely a minute away and that was good for Will. He loved surfing, loved being in the water and she loved joining him there. Anything that got Will out of his suit and into the fresh air was a plus as far as Summer was concerned.

But this place was more than she'd ever dreamt of.

The three-storey house had its original Victorian facade, and pretty balconies that took full advantage of the views across the beach and to the ocean. Behind the facade, it had been completely remodelled, though renovated sympathetic to the style, with high ceilings, classic mouldings. Traditional, but with modern touches, managing to be expansive, yet still homey and comfortable. The laundry was bigger than her old bedroom. It had more rooms than she could count.

I'm going to get lost, she thought.

'And those extra rooms in the garden, I thought that would be perfect for a recording studio.'

'What?'

'You heard me. A recording studio. For you. And, you know, in case Nina Sparrow drops by.'

Summer laughed. She'd gone to Melbourne twice to work with Nina in the past twelve months and Nina kept telling Summer she'd visit Adelaide soon. Summer had no doubt they would meet up, but have Nina visit her?

To a house like this, that would be an invitation Summer would be happy to extend.

'And now you're making so much money, it's a tax deduction.'

She smiled. He was still thinking about numbers, but that wasn't, she knew now, such a bad thing. He had helped her put aside and invest her earnings from her first contract with Nina and subsequent ones with two other artists. Summer was in demand as a songwriter, and for the first time in her life she had a steady stream of not insignificant income flowing in. The first thing on her list of things to buy was an apartment for her mother, but she wanted it to be close to wherever she and Will ended up.

'And just over the road, there's a new apartment complex.'

It was as though he'd read her mind.

'Most have sold, but there's a very nice, fully accessible one still for sale.'

'You don't think that's too close?'

'I've told you, I'd be happy for her to move in with us. It's you who has the issue with that.'

Summer loved her mother and did want to be close, but even Penny thought that living with them was a step too far. But living up the street? That could be perfect.

'Yes, you've twisted my arm.'

'Oh, have I?' Will took her hand and then spun her, pulling her towards him and into his embrace. 'You think you can manage to live here?'

'You know I can—you know it's wonderful.'

'Summer, you need to realise you belong here. You belong with me. I can't live without you. I don't want to live without you and I want to live here with you.'

It wasn't just Nina Sparrow she would be able to welcome here, but her mother, Diane, and Gus and hopefully Ben and Charlotte.

And anyone else who happened to come into their lives.

They would make this their home.

* * * * *

If you missed the previous story in the Invitation from Bali duet, then check out
Breaking the Best Friend Rule

And if you enjoyed this story, check out these other great reads from Justine Lewis

Beauty and the Playboy Prince
Back in the Greek Tycoon's World
Fiji Escape with Her Boss

All available now!

HARLEQUIN
Reader Service

Enjoyed your book?

Try the perfect subscription for Romance readers and get more great books like this delivered right to your door.

See why over 10+ million readers have tried Harlequin Reader Service.

Start with a Free Welcome Collection with free books and a gift—valued over $20.

Choose any series in print or ebook. See website for details and order today:

TryReaderService.com/subscriptions